INTRUDER FROM THE SEA

Intruder
FROM THE SEA

by GORDON McDONELL

An Atlantic Monthly Press Book

Little, Brown and Company • Boston

ATLANTIC—LITTLE, BROWN BOOKS
ARE PUBLISHED BY
LITTLE, BROWN AND COMPANY
IN ASSOCIATION WITH
THE ATLANTIC MONTHLY PRESS

Published simultaneously
in Canada by McClelland and Stewart Limited

PRINTED IN THE UNITED STATES OF AMERICA

cop 2

To SHAM and RACHEL

suaviter in modo, fortiter in re

1

It started ten years ago, right after Ploesti. Nothing made sense. When I got out of the hospital I was a civilian with perforations. Officially these were in a thighbone and a lung. To me they were ubiquitous, eyes, brain, all the senses, perforations. Life was borrowed, flat, one big hole in the sky, impertinent, unnecessary. Take it easy, they said. Take a job, they said. Do something constructive, they said. Do nothing for a while, they said. None of them said, You should have got it with all your friends. It was just Lucky Sam Freeman, that Freeman luck pulled you through, didn't it, they said.

I couldn't go home. I went home. I couldn't stay home. One day I packed a bag and caught a Greyhound at Santa Monica. I bought a ticket for San Francisco just because the bus was going there. It went up the coast highway. It was a beautiful day. The sun was shining, the sky was blue and the country was green after rain. I looked out of the windows. It was just another day.

The bus went on. It was packed full, and I sat over the rear axle. Over the vibrations. As we went on, the vibrations got worse. Malibu, Zuma, Trancas, Oxnard, Ventura, Carpenteria, Santa Barbara, Gaviota, Santa Serena.

I got out and checked my bag out. A sign said: *Santa Serena Inn, Home of Serena Soup.* I went in and asked for

1

a room, and they showed me up to the second floor. When the boy had gone I went to the window and opened it and looked out up the valley toward the pass some fifty miles away in the mountains at the end of the valley. That was the first time I had ever seen the Santa Serena valley.

I breathed in the air from the open window. It was clean and dry. It was not like the air along the coast. It was more like mountain air. It did not hurt my lung. The sea was about thirty-five miles west of here, while over the mountains to the northeast you could travel hundreds of miles over dry scrub and desert and more mountains, on and on without seeing a soul or a drop of water. The country that nearly killed my ancestors. Right here was the valley they did not find. In the sharp light I could see that the soil was richer than any I'd seen. The fields were bosoms for cattle and sheep and anything that grows. The barns were red.

I felt hungry. I turned from the window and went downstairs to the lobby. The boy who took my bag was talking with an old man in white overalls with Santa Serena Service Station on his back. Two farmers were talking together near the door. A woman tourist was sitting in an armchair, waiting for something. There was no one else in the lobby. It was the middle of the afternoon.

There was a strange kind of odor that was soothing. It seemed to come from the wood in the walls. It was a wooden hotel. I went up to the boy and asked him if it was too late to get lunch. I had not had lunch on the bus with the others because it meant getting out of the bus, and I knew that if I once got out I should not be able to get in again, so I just sat in the bus while they ate. But I did not tell the boy that. I just asked him if it was too late to get lunch.

"It is I think too late," he said. "Except, of course, for the

2

soup. We serve the soup at any time. Excuse me, I will ask my father."

He went in the back. He was a polite boy. He had a Scandinavian accent. I turned to the man in overalls.

"What is this about soup?" I asked him.

He looked at me. He was almost wizened and quite startled. He had very blue eyes with weather-beaten lines at the corners.

"Serena Soup," he said. He had a Scandinavian accent too, more pronounced than the boy's. "You do not know Serena Soup?"

I remembered the signs then, along the way. Twelve miles to Santa Serena, Home of Serena Soup. Ten miles. Eight miles. Every few miles they had one.

"I'm afraid I never tasted it. I've been out of the country. Is it new?"

He looked a little sad. He said, "You must not tell the proprietor that. He is a good friend and not to be hurt, you understand?"

"I understand."

He said, "It is not new. It has been invented now by him for the last five years. But only of late is it beginning to spread." He tapped my chest. "Young man, soon now that soup will be famous all over America. You shall see." He withdrew his hand and nodded emphatically. "In Santa Serena we all drink it. All of us."

"I look forward to tasting it," I said. "Do you rent a car by any chance?"

He looked at me carefully.

"Excuse me, but are you a foreigner?" he asked.

I looked to see if he was kidding, but his face was serious.

"What makes you think that?" I asked him.

"You said you were out of the country."

"Oh — that. No," I said. "I'm a native Californian, but

3

I've never been here before. Is this a Danish settlement?"

"That's right," he said. "Danish, but we are Americans. You plan to see the country hereabouts?"

"I'd like to."

He nodded slowly, his eyes still on my face. "It will do you good, I think. You have been to the war, perhaps?"

"Perhaps."

He caught my reaction and he put his hand on my arm. "Excuse me," he said. "I am a very rude old man."

"Not at all. You're entitled to know who you're doing business with. That is, if you have a car?"

He said, "When you have had your lunch, come over and I'll fix you up. You will find it, I think. It is called the Santa Serena Service Station. E. Andresen. Prop. That's me."

"Thank you, Mr. Andresen. My name's Freeman. I'll be right over."

We shook hands. The boy was coming back with the man who had signed me in. He was looking a little worried.

"Mr. Freeman, my son tells me you have not had your lunch. And my cook is gone to Gaviota for the afternoon. However, I can do this. I can cook you lamb chops myself. You care for that?"

"If it's too much trouble, maybe I can get something outside."

"It is not the trouble, but the selection. There is only lamb chops."

"No soup?"

He spread his hands a little. "Soup, of course, to begin."

"It's a deal. Which way do I go?"

"I will show you. If you will follow me?"

He went down some steps at the end of the lobby and through the bar. Then there was a big room with counters and little tables all over it, and little knickknacks all over the tables and counters. Little redwood souvenirs of Santa

4

Serena, dolls, dishes, table mats, glassware, post cards, all the little useless, expensive things that tourists buy and I don't. And all along one wall behind one of the counters I saw cartons containing cans. Some were quart cans and some were pint cans, all marked Serena Soup.

There was a man standing beside the counter, slitting open one of the cartons and taking some cans of soup from it. The proprietor stopped for a moment, surprised.

"Can I be of any assistance, Mr. Oakes?"

The man looked up. He was about my age, with high cheekbones and strange eyes like a cat's eyes. There was a lot of animal magnetism around him. You could feel it right away. He did not look like a Dane, I thought. From his clothes it was hard to place him, as he was just wearing blue jeans and a hunting shirt.

He said, "Oh, hullo Max, I'm taking some soup. Think I got a customer for you in Santa Barbara. Big hotel man who's coming in today. Ten hotels, eleven, something like that. How will that feel?"

He turned toward me and looked me over. I looked back at him. The proprietor, Max, seemed at a loss for a moment, then introduced us.

"Mr. Freeman, this is Mr. Oakes, one of our ranchers here. He likes to sell my soup. Mr. Freeman," he told Oakes, "is a new guest of mine and has not had his lunch yet, so I know you will excuse us."

Oakes held out his hand, so I shook it. He had a firm grip.

"I've seen your picture somewhere," he said. "Freeman. Freeman. I know. You got a medal. Flyer." He turned to Max. "He brought in a burned plane that —"

"Cut it there," I said. "Good day."

I turned and went on into the restaurant and sat down. I heard Max saying, "Mr. Oakes, next time you want soup,

5

please let me know. There is an opened carton up at the end there."

They went on about that for a moment, but I didn't listen. I sat still as I had sat in the bus, and waited for the soup. There was no one else in the restaurant and the tables were all set for dinner. I was afraid Max might come in and apologize about Oakes, but he did not.

He came back later on, bringing the soup himself. He said, "The girls are off today — it's a Danish holiday, you know. So for once I'm turning away all my highway trade, except for our hotel guests, of course."

He left me with the soup and I tasted it. After all the build-up and the mood I was in, it would have to be good. It was a fish chowder. It was not just good. It was a dream.

When he came back with the lamb chops I told him.

He nodded. "It is the turbot," he said. "By here is the only place on the coast you get turbot."

"Turbot in California? I never heard of that," I said.

"It is a smaller variety than the European species. Perhaps it took a Dane to recognize them," he laughed.

"Tell me," I said, "that Oakes — is he Danish too?"

"Johnny Oakes. No, he is no Dane. His father is much loved around here. He came from a little town on the Caspian many years ago, when they had the revolution, those Russians. I don't know his original name. He has called himself Oakes since he got here. He has one of the most beautiful ranches in the valley. A wonderful man, old Andrew." He sighed. "Johnny does not take after him. I'm sorry if he annoyed you."

I said, "It was nothing."

He left me to eat, and I thought about the valley and the turbot and the Danes and the Oakeses, and finished my lunch and went into the lobby. Johnny Oakes was talking to the boy at the desk. He had two of the quart cans of soup

6

under his arm. He turned to me as I went to the desk and smiled. It was a strange smile, as though he was doing his best with it with his lips, but his eyes could not make it although they were trying.

He said, "How did you like the soup?"

"Fine, thanks," I said. I said to the boy at the desk, "Please tell your father those were the best lamb chops I've had in years, will you? I'll be back this evening."

"Thank you, sir," the boy said. "I will tell him."

I turned to go out the door, but Johnny Oakes was standing between me and the door now, still smiling in that uncertain kind of way of his, and he said, "I'm sorry if I offended you just now."

I said, "The fault was mine, I guess. Let's skip it, shall we?"

"That's very good of you. Arvid here tells me you are going to rent a car and plan to see our valley?"

I said, "Quite a grapevine you have here."

He laughed, waving a hand. "You know how it is — small place." He was walking along beside me now as I made for the door. "What about the gas rationing?"

I looked at him.

"I hadn't thought of it. But the old man said he'd fix me up, so I guess he has ways."

"Yeah, I guess he can for you."

We were walking up the street now, leading off the main highway. I could see the station at the corner of the block. There were only three blocks altogether, so it was simple to find. Simpler than shaking Johnny Oakes. I thought I could tell him to go jump a river, but then I thought it was good discipline not to, so I just walked along.

He said, "In that case, I was wondering if you could do me a favor."

"Drop you off some place, you mean?"

"Not me. A can of soup. My father wants some soup, and I have to go to Santa Barbara. You want to see the valley, and this way you can see our ranch. It's a fine ranch. Would you mind very much?"

"Is it far?"

"No."

"All right, then. Give me the soup and the directions."

He was very grateful. He gave me a can, and then drew a little map on the back of an envelope and marked it with an X.

"Right here on the right-hand side of the road. There's a sign. It says RED BARNS. You can't miss it."

"The sign or the barns?"

He grinned.

"The sign." He started to turn away, and then he added, "If my father's not around, just leave it with my sister, will you?"

He waved his hand and was walking away before I could answer. I shrugged to myself and went over to Andresen's place. There was nobody about, but there was an old Chevvy standing in front of the pumps with a note on the windshield. It said, "Mr. Freeman, in case I'm not back when you come, take this car. Settle when you return. E. Andresen."

I put the note in my pocket, and smiled and got in the car and headed the way Johnny Oakes had told me. I had a good feeling as I drove along, looking at the valley. It got more and more beautiful. When I got near the place Johnny described, I started looking around.

The place was not hard to find, because of the sign. Without it, any one of the ranches around might have been called Red Barns. I was wondering to myself who had thought up the name as I drove in through the gate and over the cattle bars. I had an instant feeling that it must

8

have been the old man, because, partly, of the way Max had spoken of him.

There had been a gentleness in Max's voice as he spoke of the old man, and, looking about me as I drove up the winding little road to the ranch house, the feeling of peace and security and dignity and quiet was confirmed in everything I saw. The little wooden bridge over the creek, unfenced, with four gleaming white tubs standing one at each corner, the watercress in the creek bed, the willows beside it, the paddock of brood mares, the notice at the top of the hill from the creek as the driveway entered the circle before the house itself, PLEASE DRIVE SLOW, and everywhere, in all the fields, and in the garden right beside the house, the great live oaks, many of them with attendant trails of Spanish moss about them, all of them old, peaceful, serene.

There was a fenced-in permanent pasture in front of the house, and the driveway circled around it. A young black filly was standing in the pasture with her head over the fence, eating a carrot that a girl was holding out to her.

The girl was wearing jeans and Western boots and a gray jacket, and she had no hat. Her hair was long and dark brown and shining and tied with a ribbon at the back. She and the filly watched me as I got out of the car and went up to them, and I saw that the girl was about twenty or so, and she had been crying.

She was not crying now any more, but she had been crying not so very long ago. There was a puffiness under the eyes, which were overly bright still from the recent tears, and there was a listlessness that seemed foreign to her nature. Normally you would say here was a girl who was on the ball and commanding.

I did not wish to intrude, but there I was. I took off my

9

hat. The filly shied violently and sped away in a sudden gallop. We both watched her as she went in outraged ecstasy, shining black, kicking up her heels as she galloped, apparently headed straight for a crack-up against the fence on the other side. Somehow she swerved and braked, reared up, and as suddenly was standing perfectly still again, only now upon the other side of the pasture.

The girl turned back to me. The listlessness was gone.

"You can put your hat on again now. And keep it on."

"I'm sorry I scared her. I thought she was going to break her neck for a minute."

"I'd have broken yours if she had. But don't worry — she does it all the time. You haven't been around horses much, have you?"

"Not much."

"What do you want?"

I ignored the tone of her question. It was better to see her spirit back, even if a little sharpened by her need to conceal her troubles from a stranger.

I said, "I've brought some soup for Mr. Oakes." I held out the can to her. "I met Johnny Oakes, and he asked me to bring this over for him as he had to go to Santa Barbara. He said to see you if Mr. Oakes wasn't around — that is, if you are his sister."

She did not look like his sister at all, I thought, but she took the can.

"Thank you. Did he say when he would be back from Santa Barbara?"

"No, but I heard him say something to the owner of the inn that he knew of a big customer for him there, so he might be late, I'd say."

She looked thoughtful, and privately distressed, but then she recovered herself and said, "And you came all this way to bring a can of soup, Mr. — er — ?"

10

"Freeman. Sam Freeman. That's all right. I wanted to see the country around here anyway, so he asked me if I'd do it for him."

"See the country?"

She looked at me, and for a moment I thought she was going to ask about the gas rationing, but she didn't. I saw that she was still concerned with her own troubles by the way her eyes were looking at me, yet not seeming to notice me.

She said, "In that case, Mr. Freeman, maybe you have time to help me catch the filly again before you go? I'll have to get all the horses in by myself today."

"Be glad to help. You'll have to explain things."

She smiled for the first time. "Just no sudden movements."

We both laughed. The tension was gone. She put the can on a fencepost. "Remind me to pick it up when we're through. Dad will want it when he wakes up." She picked up a halter and handed me a bunch of carrots. "These will help you," she said. "We'll go in. Every time I try to put the halter on from outside she ducks away."

I opened the gate and we went in, and I closed the gate behind us. The filly saw the carrots and started toward me, and then she saw the halter in the girl's hands and sheered away. It was so transparent it made us laugh. The girl had nice teeth when she laughed, white and even, not like Johnny's teeth. His were a little irregular and crowded together. I thought, Two hours ago, Freeman, you were sitting in a bus feeling awful and now you're laughing with a girl trying to catch a horse.

She was calling to the filly. "Here Jilly girl, come now, here Jilly." The filly took no notice at all.

"That her name, Jilly?"

"Her name's Black Jill really, but we call her Jilly."

"What's your name?"

She looked at me.

"Me? Oh, I'm Liza."

The laughter had suddenly gone out of her face and it was strange the way she said it, almost as if she hated herself. But it only lasted an instant, that impression, and then it was gone as the filly caught her eye again.

"Watch out," Liza called, "she'll get all the carrots."

Black Jill had sneaked up on me and I pulled the bunch away from her as her lips were curling over it. I took one carrot and held it out to her gently and she took it without noticing Liza with the halter. Then Liza had her arm around the filly's neck and started saying things in her ear and putting on the halter and Black Jill stood perfectly still and quiet now. I opened the gate and Liza led her along behind us. We walked across the driveway up toward two red barns and a long low building of stables, also red.

"It's a little early yet to bring the horses in," Liza said. "But I've so much to do I can't help it. Today's a Danish holiday and the two men we have are away. They're both as old as the hills anyway." There was, I thought, a shade of undertone in her inflection, and I wanted to ask why Johnny wasn't there but I didn't.

"How many horses have you got?"

She began to count on her fingers. She had beautifully proportioned hands with long fingers, and she kept her nails quite short for a woman and without any color.

"Nine altogether," she said, "if you count poor old Cherry and Cassandra." She pointed over to the field beyond the stableyard. Two gray horses were quietly grazing under a tree. Their coats had long ceased to be coats, but were thick, long-haired fur. "They're almost thirty now. They don't come in at night. Dad got them originally just

12

for riding around the ranch. I used to ride them when I was little."

"What are the others?"

"Black Mark, his two wives, Nightshade and Eyewash, and Black Jack and Black Jill, both out of Nightshade; and then there's Blackeye out of Eyewash."

"You mean they're all black horses?"

"Well, Blackeye and Eyewash aren't completely, but the rest are. It isn't that I breed them because they're black, but simply that Black Mark's line has always had lots of black and Nightshade is closely related to him, same line through the grandsire."

"Is that good?"

"Look at Jill. And in a moment you'll see Jack. I believe in it very much. Look at breeders like the Aga Khan and Boussac. That's one of their secrets. In fact, I think I'm going to breed Jill to Mark in another three or four years."

"Sounds to me like you might get a crazy horse."

"You double your chances of getting all the bad qualities or all the good. I might get a superhorse."

"Suppose it turns out the other way?"

"I can have it shot." She stopped beside the big round water trough in the middle of the stableyard and turned to the filly. "Water, Jilly girl, nice water, Jilly girl." Her voice was gentle and coaxing again now and the filly almost immediately began to drink. The transformation in the girl in one short second was quite something. From an incisive woman horse breeder to a little girl with a filly.

I said, "Don't your father and your brother have anything to say about that?"

She gave me a level look. "You're certainly direct, aren't you?"

"I'm sorry. I guess I lost my manners lately. You'd best just put me to work."

13

The filly stopped drinking and put up her head, the water dripping from her chin. We started walking again, up to one of the stalls.

Liza said, "No, it's a good question. I guess I do sound a little strange the way I talk. The answer is that Dad himself doesn't know much about horses, but he believes in my flair for thoroughbreds and so he lets me manage them."

She opened the door to the stall and took off Black Jill's halter and gave her a slap on the fanny and the filly went into the stall.

I said, "And what about your brother, doesn't he take an interest in them?"

She slid back the bolt separating the top half of the door.

"No," she said. "Johnny doesn't care for horses. Not at all." She closed the lower half of the door and bolted it. "Three doors up is the tack room. You'll find a bunch of halters just inside the door on your right. Do you mind? Then I can be fixing the feed."

"You bet," I said. I turned obediently and went up three doors and opened the door and went in. I was still thinking about the tone of her voice when she had answered me about Johnny as I went in, and then, while I looked around, I forgot about it as I took in the surroundings of the tack room. I had expected a roomful of tack. Just that, nothing more. But this room took my breath away. It was as clean and shipshape as an army barracks ready for inspection. The concrete floor was swept clean, the redwood walls were without dust, and on the walls hung rows of polished bits, halters, reins, pieces of gear for horses that I knew nothing about, saddles neatly arranged on racks, everything stacked in order. There were racing photographs on the walls, and a diamond-quartered cap and jacket hung under crossed whips. You could see that a lot of love had

14

gone into that room. I went up and examined some of the photographs. They had all been taken shortly before the war, when racing ceased. One of them had been taken long before. A black horse winning a race, big crowds a blur in the background. Underneath it said, Black Mark, Saratoga, some date in the thirties that I couldn't quite read.

Liza's voice behind me said, "That was the last time he ran."

I turned. She was looking at the picture, too.

She said, "I saw that race. I saw him go lame right after. I was a little girl. I begged Dad for him. I knew he was a great horse. Dad got him cheap because they didn't know it. I knew he'd turn out a great sire. But now I can't prove it till racing starts again. After the war."

"Too bad," I said. I went over to what looked like halters at the right of the door where she had told me and picked them up. "Hadn't we better get going? You said there was lots to do."

She flushed. All over her face. She came over in two quick steps and stood there in front of me, her breasts nearly bursting out of the gray jacket-sweater garment she had on. She looked awful cute. For a moment I thought maybe she might hit me, but she decided against it.

She said, "All right, so you just got back from the war. You think I didn't guess that the moment I saw you? But what do you expect me to do — shoot all my horses?"

I shrugged. "Well, horses are horses. But I guess someone has to look after them, though. Okay, let's go."

"You still don't understand, or won't. Look. You don't think that's all I do, do you? On this ranch we grow food, just like any other. The horses I spend a minimum of time with. Now, do you get it?"

I said, "I'm sorry, Liza. I hadn't thought of that. But you

15

could have explained it to me, you know, step by step. I'm pretty simple."

We had both recovered again now. She smiled.

"Come on then, simple Sam."

There was something about her though, that I still did not get. It was something about the way she was over all this breeding-horses business. It just did not seem to sit for a girl her age, not unless she had been brought up to it, that is. And she had just said that she had not, that it was all her own idea. As I followed her out and walked along beside her to the paddocks and we got the horses in together, talking of trivial matters, I gradually ceased to wonder about it, seeing more and more the way she had with the animals; she had, as she had said, a flair for them, and I decided that that was probably the simple explanation, she had been born with it, just as some are born with a flair for the violin. Perhaps it was not that aspect which was puzzling me at all, I thought, remembering the evidence of tears.

The afternoon wind had died down completely as we brought in Black Jack. By that time I had become enough of an expert to do it myself, and when I had bolted his stall and left him to his feed, I saw that Liza was listless again.

"Now I have the farm chores," she said. "Thank you so much for your help."

"That part of it bores you, doesn't it?"

"Bores?" She closed the lid on the grain bin and came to the doorway where I was standing. "I guess that's it," she said, and I knew somehow it wasn't that at all. We went out into the stableyard again.

"What about Black Mark? Doesn't he have to be brought in too?"

She looked at me and laughed.

16

"You don't lead a stud around. At least not Black Mark. Come, I'll show you where he lives."

We walked along the row of stalls and around the big barn at the far end. There was a little more spring to her now, I thought, as we walked toward the stallion's place. He had a building all to himself with a big stall in it and a peaked roof. Under the triangle of the roof there was a plaque above the outside door which read: *Black Mark. By Night Owl out of Valkyr by Man o' War.* Even I had heard of the last name. There was another door, standing open, that led from the stall to the paddock, which was a big one, all for him, so he could come and go as he wished. At the moment he was standing at the far side of the paddock, looking across at the two gray ghosts under the tree. He turned and saw us and came at a run.

"Cassandra drives him crazy so watch out," Liza said. "The war has cheated him on his love life, poor old boy."

He didn't look like a poor old boy as he came at me, I thought. He reared up on his hind legs and bared his teeth and started thrashing down with his forelegs, and I began to wonder if the fence was high enough. We were standing too close to the fence but the girl did not move back so I could not either.

"Quit that, Mark," she shouted at him. "Quit that stuff."

He came down again and started tossing his head with his teeth still bared and I began to get the feeling that he was putting on an act because of her.

I said, "If you weren't here, he'd have mashed me up by now."

She was looking at me.

"You could have moved back a little," she said. There was a light in her eyes now that I had not seen before, as if she was seeing me for the first time. She handed me a carrot.

"Here, give him one, and watch it."

I held out the carrot at arm's length. He came at it with all his teeth and made a vicious jab, cutting it clean in half. Suddenly I got mad. I don't know why, but it just made me mad, that a fool horse should act that way. I threw the other half of the carrot in his face as hard as I could.

"The heck with you," I shouted at him. He backed off.

Suddenly she began to laugh. She threw her head back and really laughed. It was good to see.

"Any time you need a job, you're hired," she said.

I said, "Lady, I wouldn't go inside that fence for a barrel of monkeys. I suppose you go in all the time?"

"He's all right when you're inside. I don't know why but he is. It's just he likes to rush at people on the other side of the fence."

"Perhaps he's jealous they're outside and he's not."

She said, "You do know about horses after all."

"All I know is they're darn dangerous at both ends and very uncomfortable in the middle, as I read somewhere. Why doesn't your brother help you on the ranch?"

Her whole face changed, as though the sun had gone in.

"If you mean with the horses, I told you he doesn't like them. He does lots of farming. Why do you ask that?" She looked at me thoughtfully a moment, then said, "I suppose it's natural, because you saw him selling soup. The answer is, though I don't know it's any of your business, that he thinks there is going to be a lot of money in that soup and he's trying to horn in on it."

We were walking back now, toward the front of the house where we had first met.

I said, "Well, unless he has some special pull with Max I don't think he'll get far."

"What makes you say that?" Her voice was low but very distinct.

18

I said, "Just an impression. I'm sorry, I shouldn't be talking like this."

"Since you are," she said, "you might as well finish."

"Well then, frankly, I don't think Max likes him."

She stopped walking and stood looking at me. I waited for her to speak. There was a faraway kind of look in her face, like the time I first saw her with the filly when I told her he had gone to Santa Barbara.

She said, "Nobody likes Johnny. Including you. Tell me, why did you do what he asked?"

"I don't really know the answer to that. It wasn't as if I were putting myself out anyway."

"You did something for someone you disliked on sight. Isn't that unusual?"

She really wanted to know.

I said, "Well, there was something about him. I don't quite know how to describe it, but somehow I found it hard to refuse him. Almost as if he was a child that would take a refusal as a sign of disapproval."

Suddenly she laughed. It wasn't like the other laugh, but hard and bitter.

"That's a good one. That's a very good one."

The door of the house opened and a man came out. He was an old man, but as he came down the path toward us I could see at once that he was Johnny's father.

Liza said, "Hello, Dad. This is Mr. Freeman. He's staying at Max's. He was kind enough to bring you some soup. He met Johnny in town."

He shook hands. He was a very courteous old man. That was the immediate impression I got of him, that and his brittleness. It was not the brittleness of extreme old age, for he was not as old as that, but a certain texture of the skin from some malfunctioning of his body. Although he had the contours of face that Johnny had, the eyes and the

19

general mien were quite different. It was like looking at the obverse side of a coin, I thought. If you discounted the age difference, here was what Johnny ought to have been. The strength and the charm were there, without the weakness or the evil or whatever it was about Johnny that emanated from him.

I said, "I'm glad to meet you, sir."

He said, "How do you do, Mr. Freeman. It was kind of you. I hope my daughter has shown you around?"

"Indeed she has, thanks."

He nodded and turned to Liza. "So he is at Max's still?"

She said, "That's all right, Dad, I can manage."

"I wonder if he saw Svenson about the sheep. I think I call Svenson — but no, it would be useless before his suppertime." He sighed. "And then maybe too late."

Liza said, "Look, Dad, I was just going to call on the off chance he's in. You fix your soup now. Here, take it."

He took the can from her and smiled at me. You could see how he loved her to boss him around.

He said, "You are staying long at the inn?"

"I don't rightly know. I only just got in today. Maybe I'll stay quite a while. I'm recuperating from the war."

I wondered why I had volunteered that. It wasn't like me at all. There must be something special about this old man, I thought.

He nodded and said, "Is a good place as any for that." Then he gave a laugh. "I've been recuperating here twenty-six years so I should know." We all laughed because he was laughing and he nodded his head again. "Twenty-six years."

I said, "What's with the sheep?"

"Dipping, just dipping. Tomorrow we dip them, the little rascals. If I can get Svenson. I need his tank. We take

20

his tank, he takes our cat, you know how it is among farmers."

"If you can't get him on the phone maybe I could drive over to his place with a message?"

"If you do that," the old man said, "you will stay for supper when you get back. Isn't that right, Liza?"

"As long as he doesn't mind scratch cooking of mine tonight. But first let me call and see if he's in the house or not. There's a chance."

2

We all went in the house together. The old man wanted to show me things, but Liza shooed him into the kitchen to fix his soup. He always had to have soup when he finished his sleep, she explained. She asked me to wait while she went to the telephone.

I waited in the living room. The telephone was in one of the bedrooms. The living room was the sort of living room that you don't see much any more. It was fusty and Victorian, and yet it had a charm of its own in spite of the strange knickknacks here and there that made it seem like a woman's room in a way. Victorian was not the right word because of the continental air it had from such things as an ikon on the wall and a battered old samovar on a little table between the windows. But what made the room was the huge fireplace and the wonderful view from the windows, looking out over the rolling green and brown fields with the great oaks and the sheep. The gentleness of it made you sigh deep down with relief at coming home from the bustle of a modern world into a life that you read about in books of more pastoral days.

There were two old-fashioned portraits hanging on the wall opposite the fireplace. One of them I recognized at once as the old man, but it had been taken when he was much younger. He looked about forty in the picture. His hair was black, like Johnny's. The other was a woman in her early thirties. She was looking directly into the camera with an expression of great candor and simplicity and she had a vague resemblance to Johnny somewhere but I could not quite place it.

I crossed the room to look more closely at the picture, and I saw that her lips were not quite so full as I had at first imagined and there was a slight cast in the left eye, although the lighting of the photograph, which was not good, might have been the cause of this. She had the same high cheekbones as Johnny and the old man, and her hair also was black. She was not quite what you would call a beautiful woman, but on the other hand her face had too much character to be called pretty. Judging purely from the face you could not tell what her nature was. She might have been a very lovable woman of great charm, or on the other hand she might have been one who did not associate easily with people at all. I wondered why I was trying to analyze her so carefully and then I realized that I had been looking for some likeness to Liza, but I could find none.

I could hear Liza's voice on the telephone, speaking in a low tone, but I could not hear the words. The old man came into the room eating his soup out of a bowl as he walked along, and his eyes twinkled at me over the top of it.

"Liza does not like me to walk with my soup," he said, "but it is a thing I have always enjoyed to do ever since I was a boy. It has probably ruined my digestion." He smiled widely and nodded at the picture of the woman beside me. "That was my wife, Maria. She died five years ago. She was the most wonderful woman in the world. She even let me walk with my soup when we had no company although she did not care for it, I think. So to please her I would not do it if we had company. Sit down, young man, and relax yourself."

He took the armchair by the fireplace although he still had not finished his soup.

I sat down, and said, "Max at the inn told me you came over here from the Caspian."

"That is right. It is odd, is it not, for a fisherman to become a farmer? But then in a way I was always something of both in our little town. We had a small farm by the sea, close by the town. It was really a village, but we always called it a little town."

He put down his soup bowl and looked across at the picture of Maria, and then he started to talk as though he was reminding her of those old days instead of telling me.

"Sometimes in the winter, in January and February, we would go out upon the ice. The sea would be frozen over so thick you could go out upon the ice with many horses and sleighs. Perhaps a hundred men would go, bringing axes and nets. Then with the axes we would cut great holes in the ice and lower the nets down. When we would pull up the nets, what did we have, eh? Sturgeon, yes such fine sturgeon as you could find anywhere in Russia, for it was their spawning time nearly, and they were awaiting the thaw to take them up the Volga or the Ural or the Emba. Once, I remember when the thaw came early, and we were still upon the ice which was beginning to separate and drift. There was still one passage of ice left open to the shore. But we were so many sleighs that it looked as if —"

Liza came into the room and was now standing waiting for him to finish his story, and he knew this and stopped.

He said, "I am a garrulous old man. Be off now to the chores. What of the tank?"

Liza said, "Svenson was in the house, so I chatted with him. He says Johnny did not go for the tank but we can

24

have it if we can send for it somehow, but I told him Johnny has the truck."

There was a silence that you could feel.

The old man said, "His men are all away today of course."

I said, "Why can't I get it?"

"How could you?" she asked. "Unless you have a trailer hitch on that car? Then we could load the tank on our trailer."

"Let's look."

We went out to look at the car, the three of us. There was no hitch on it.

"Can't Svenson drive it over himself?" I asked. "Doesn't he have a truck?"

The old man's face hardened visibly. It was the first time he had shown his feelings so clearly.

He said, abruptly for him, "I will not for a moment do this. He would not ask such a thing of me if his son had done the same. We will postpone the dip a day."

"I could drive over, bring the tank on his truck, take the truck back and get my car."

The old man laughed, his face suddenly clearing in the instant. He slapped me on the back.

"It's twenty miles to Svenson's place. Forget about it."

Liza said, "If we're not doing the sheep tomorrow then I'll get the hay started now. Then we'll have a full day to finish tomorrow."

"Fan belt's busted on the cat," the old man said. "You'd have to fix it first. I've got to finish my accounts for that inspector. You best just do the hogs and let it go."

I said, "Fan belts are my department. You got a spare?"

The old man chuckled.

"You better show him where it is, Liza. He's determined

to earn his supper." He grinned at me and turned and went back in the house.

Liza said, "That's very nice of you. I'll show you where it is. Are you good with machines?"

"Not an expert, but I was a flyer."

"Oh," she said.

She walked on a way in silence. We were headed for the shed, behind the garage. I could see the tractor standing under the roof outside the shed.

She said, "Were you in Africa?"

"Little time, yes."

"You didn't get to Abyssinia did you?"

"No. Why?"

"I just wondered. I knew some people who were lost there once." She reached up to a shelf running along the wall of the shed and took down a carton half full of odds and ends. "There's a fan belt in here somewhere," she said. "Here it is." She handed it to me. "I hope it's the right size."

I looked at it and compared it with the one on the motor.

"Looks okay to me. Got a wrench?"

"All the tools are over here, bench tools, jacks, planes, lathes, drills — there's even a gadget for sealing up tin cans around somewhere."

"Sounds like you don't care for machinery?"

"You know what I like."

"You like horses, Johnny likes machinery, and I like both. How's that?"

"Not bad for a beginner. I'll be over with the pigs, by the other barn. Give a yell when you're through, will you?"

She turned without waiting for an answer. I started in on the fan belt, wondering about the Oakes family. There seemed a lot of charge in the air.

When I had got the belt fixed, I checked over the oil and water and gas. Then I started the motor to see how it ran.

26

It was not as smooth as it could have been. I switched it off and climbed down off the high seat and got a rag and a wrench and started to check the plugs. They were well used. I looked around to see if I could find a new set, and after a lot of hunting, I found some. I unwrapped them and put them in the motor. Then I climbed up and started the motor again. This time it was all right. As I was listening to the sound of it running, I heard Johnny's voice calling "Hullo."

He had drawn up alongside in a truck. He had a big tank roped onto the truck. I switched off the cat's motor.

He was smiling.

"Hullo," I said.

"Hoped you'd still be around," he said.

"Thought you'd gone to Santa Barbara."

"Man's flight was canceled. That motor sounds better. You changed the plugs as well as the fan belt, didn't you?"

I nodded. "You must have made good time from Svenson's place. Your sister called only half an hour ago, maybe a little more."

"I know, I got there just after." He laughed. "I drive too fast."

He jumped down from the truck. He was perfectly at ease and the movements of his body were smooth and sure. Lithe. He stood looking at the motor of the tractor.

"You did a nice job," he said.

"Thanks."

"You know, I'd been planning to do that the past few days. I like to fool around with motors, don't you?"

"Not particularly. But flyers depend on their motors a lot."

He laughed again.

"Often thought I'd like to fly," he said. He took out a

27

pack of Chesterfields from his shirt pocket, and offered me one.

"Not right now, thanks. I'm trying to cut down."

He lit his cigarette.

"How d'you like our place?" he asked.

"Very much indeed." I jumped down from the tractor seat. "Your sister asked me to let her know when I was through so I could help her with whatever's to be done. But now, since you're back —"

"Oh, stick around, do," he interrupted me quickly. "It's been very kind of you to do what you have, but I'm sure you can't have seen over the whole place yet. There's lots to show you and, for that matter," he laughed, "plenty to do too if it comes to that. I was hoping that maybe you might like to stay to supper with us?"

I didn't like him, and I'm not considered by my friends to have a weak character; but for some reason, which I could not have analyzed, I hesitated.

He said quickly, "Besides, I want you to meet my father."

"We met just now," I said.

"Grand. How did you get on together?"

"Just fine."

"I'm sure he'd be disappointed if you didn't stay."

He waved over my shoulder and I turned and saw Liza coming across the yard toward us.

"I was just telling Freeman he must stay for supper, Liza. He seems to think he should go because I came back."

She looked at Johnny a moment, a level expressionless look, and then she looked at me. The charge was in the air now and no mistaking it.

She said, "Of course you're staying — you said you would."

Her tone was urgent. Almost as though she needed help.

28

"It doesn't look as if I could get away if I tried," I said. "What do we do next?"

"That's something we're never quite sure of around here," she said. "What do you suggest, Johnny?"

He didn't like it. Even I could see that. He stared at her, right in the eyes.

He said, "We'll fix up the tank together. You get the supper. Then we'll be ready when you are."

"Yes, Johnny." She turned to me. "See you later," she said, and walked off toward the house without another word.

I lit a cigarette.

"Where do you want the tank?" I asked him.

He climbed in the truck.

"Jump in," he said. "I'll show you."

I got in beside him and he started up. He drove across the yard and through an open gate into the field behind the big barn. There was a corral and an animal chute set up there with wattling and a pit for the tank at the end of the ramp. It was all set up, ready for the tank. He drove across the field toward the corral.

He said, "We're leaving this field fallow this year. We always use the closest fallow one for the dip. Sometimes do it in the yard, but Liza doesn't care for that because of the horses."

"You mean she can influence your decision?"

He looked at me and laughed.

"Not mine," he said, "but my father's."

He pulled up the truck by the tank pit, still chuckling. I got out of the truck, and took off my coat.

He said, "There's some sacking here you could tie around your waist to protect those trousers."

"Thanks, but they're due for cleaning anyway."

I started untying the rope. He went to work on his

end. He explained about leaving the rope under the tank and paying it out top and bottom till we had a good pull on it.

"That way, if we're lucky, the tank will turn as we pull and land right way up in the pit. Sometimes it does and sometimes it doesn't. Ready?"

I watched him and imitated his pull as best I could. The tank flipped over and landed in the pit. He laughed like a kid.

"See? It worked. That means we're in luck this year."

Somehow I just couldn't help smiling at the man. He radiated his feelings in a strange animal fashion. One minute he was up, one minute down, but always unpredictable. I put on my coat and we got back in the truck and headed back to the shed. A strange sensation began to steal over me, as though I had done a good day's work. For the first time since I could remember I found I had lost my feeling of tension within. The sun was just setting as we put the truck in and walked toward the house. In that light the whole place took on a sharp and colored clarity that was very beautiful. Johnny must have sensed something of my mood for he said, "It's a long way to go, back to the inn and back, if you're coming to the dip. Why don't you stay here?"

"Aren't you jumping your fences? I haven't said anything about coming back."

"You will, I think."

It was strange the way he said it, not in an arrogant way but a prophetic one. What the Irish call second sight. It gave me a strange feeling, although by now I was becoming used to having strange feelings about Johnny Oakes. He unlatched the gate to the front garden and held it for me to go through.

"Incidentally," he said, "you're not married, are you?"

That one really threw me. I stopped in the gateway and frankly stared at him.

"It happens I'm not. Why do you ask?"

He waved me on and casually flicked the gate shut.

"Why, just to make sure I wasn't omitting your wife, of course." He pointed to some tall blue flowers growing against the house by the front door. "You don't happen to know what those things are called do you? I never can remember names of flowers."

"I wouldn't know."

"You too." He laughed. He was very poised and care-free as he opened the door to the house. "We'll have to wait for someone to come along who does. Nobody around here knows much about flowers. Come on in."

The living room was empty. I could hear sounds coming from the direction of the kitchen.

"I expect my father is doing accounts," Johnny said.

"That's what he said he had to do."

"Oh. Well, we won't disturb him till it's time to eat. Come and see my room."

I followed him through the door leading off to the right, opposite the one that led to the dining room and kitchen. We went down a corridor, past a big master bedroom. The door was left wide open and I could see a huge old-fashioned four-poster bed complete with its lace curtains looped back at the head, and a big picture of Maria on the little table beside the bed. There was a door half open on the far side of the room through which I could hear the sounds of a typewriter. Johnny went on down a couple of steps in the corridor and opened a door at the end and stood aside.

"Come in," he said. "This is my room."

The walls were black. That is to say, the base of the pattern was black, if you could call it a pattern exactly.

31

It was rather a scheme than a pattern. Scattered over the black background, in an almost feverish disorder, were masks, done in red, green and orange, and also varying sizes of circular white dots, and light blue dots and cerise dots, from dinner-plate size to a half dollar.

I could feel his eyes on my face, watching for my reaction, and I wondered what to say. There was a divan bed in the middle of the room and the usual bedroom furnishing except for a small desk in one corner. The furniture was all the painted modern variety, in complete contrast to the rest of the house furniture, in complete contrast to the house. I did not even get the impression that it was well done.

He said, "You don't like it, do you?"

"Well, I think it might be hard getting to sleep."

He laughed.

"I didn't expect you to like it. I could see you were attracted to the rest of the house."

There was no sarcasm or irony in his tone although the words sounded that way. He said them quite straight, and somehow that made it sadder, that he took for granted nowadays, after whatever long time it takes to take such a thing for granted — the fact that he was different from the rest of his own family even, let alone the rest of mankind.

And yet, did he? The mere fact that he had wanted me to see the room, the studied fury of those walls, didn't that mean a revolt against taking it for granted? Such speculations were a little out of my depth, and as we returned to the living room, and he was telling me of various scenic spots in the valley that I should visit, I decided that it was no use my trying to figure him out.

Liza came in wearing a black dress, loose fitting, and her hair was up now and drawn tight about her head, and her ears were showing. She had a beautiful head and small ears; the dress seemed to me somehow out of style, although I could not have said just how, but when the eye fell on the ankles you forgave her the dress right away.

She said, "Dinner's ready anytime from now on. Would you care for a drink first?"

"Of course he would," Johnny said. "I'll fix one while you tell Dad."

"Not for me, thanks," I said. And I could have done with a drink at that, but that was Johnny for you, always rubbing me up the wrong way. Yet he couldn't have been more genial. So now Johnny fixed himself a whisky, and Liza came back in with the old man.

At first his gaze passed over me. He had forgotten I was coming, as he saw Johnny with a drink, but in the same instant he caught sight of me, beamed in his courtly way, and said, "Liza, get the Smirnoff and the black cucumber and we will make toast."

Liza smiled at him and touched his wrist.

"Look, Dad, Mr. Freeman already said No, and you know the last time you took vodka you got sick, and I don't drink it nowadays so —"

The old man laughed, looking at me.

"It is true then?"

I said, "Thank you, sir. Johnny already offered me one."

"In that case," he said with a brief glance at Johnny, "we shall proceed to our victuals when Johnny is ready."

Johnny waved his hand.

"I'm ready. Don't wait on me."

He drained his glass and set it down. The old man ushered me in behind Liza.

The dining room was in the same style as the living room, old-fashioned, clean and comfortable, with no pretensions to anything special. There was a side table against

33

the wall that looked as if it had come out of the ark, and possibly had. A grandfather clock ticked in the corner. Liza had drawn the curtains across the windows and put candles on the table. The candles were new and very long and I suspected they were in my honor. And also there were plenty of flowers on the table, the tall blue ones Johnny had pointed out and some smaller white ones surrounding them. She had made the table really pretty.

We all sat down, the old man at the head of the table and Liza at the foot. I sat on the old man's right and Johnny sat opposite me. Liza had made a salad and served a casserole of chicken with mushrooms and garlic and wine. The old man tasted it carefully and I could see at once that he was used to good food, the way he appraised it for a moment and then nodded at Liza, who was awaiting this as though it were a regular ritual. Johnny just dived straight in. He did not seem to notice anything about what was on his plate.

I said, "This chicken is delicious. I've never had it quite this way."

Liza smiled and the old man smiled too and said, "There are many ways of cooking chicken. I think sometimes my Maria taught her better than she realized." He turned to Liza, "No saffron today?"

Liza said, "Last time you had too much saffron even though I only put in a pinch. You said it spoiled the wine flavor. So this time I put in orégano and sweet basil and rosemary."

"And garlic," Johnny said.

"Yes, Johnny, and pepper and salt. Can you taste that too, maybe?"

The old man looked up quickly from his plate at Liza and I got the feeling he was a little surprised at the quickness in her tone, and a little distressed too.

34

He said, "Sometimes, of course, a dish can become too spicy, Lizakin."

She flushed a little and her eyes became suddenly like a spaniel's eyes as she looked at him and said, "Oh, Dad, I'm sorry you don't like it."

"Of course I like it," he said at once. "There is no question." He turned to me. "You see," he explained, "I think my stomach is at last beginning to rebel against a long lifetime with saffron and my palate has not yet informed my brain of this fact. But Liza remembers." He laughed suddenly, as though dispelling all evil humors. "It does not do to argue with a woman about cooking, if she knows the men she is cooking for."

Johnny said, "Chicken's okay, but I've always thought it's rather a woman's dish, haven't you?"

For a moment I had not realized he was addressing me until Liza said, "His name is Sam."

Johnny shot her an interested look at this, which I just caught as I looked up from my plate.

I said, "Depends how hungry you are, I guess. Personally I had a late lunch and I've done little since, so it suits me just fine." I smiled at Liza and repeated, "Just fine."

Johnny smiled, self-satisfied.

"That's right, you did have a late lunch." He turned to the old man. "I met Sam at Max's place this afternoon. He said he wanted to see the country so I sent him with the soup. Do you think we can keep him?"

The old man looked at me and twinkled and said, "No. He has not the farm in his blood."

I said, "I guess that's right. I'll end up in the city. But the farm is good for a change."

"You come from Los Angeles?" the old man asked.

"Santa Monica. Born and raised there, except for two years at school in the East. The war stopped that."

35

"Do you plan to resume?"

"I don't know, Mr. Oakes, what I plan right now. Hard to have any plans. I guess I'll probably go to work in Los Angeles some place. Business management, insurance, stocks, something like that, maybe. Just so long as it's within reach of the ocean."

"You are a fisherman?"

"Surfboard is my specialty, but I do quite a bit of fishing."

"Then you must see our lake. It is something to fish."

"You have a lake on the ranch?"

"Yes, in the mountains. Just twenty minutes on a horse."

"Well, I can just ride a horse, but I've no fishing rod with me."

Johnny said, "There's fishing equipment in the boathouse. Liza can take you up, can't you, Liza? After all, it's your lake."

She did not look at him, but she flushed a little as she looked at me and said, "He means I like to paint it. It's very lovely."

I said, "You paint too? I'd like to see some of your work."

Johnny said, "You'd much better see the lake. She puts in every duck."

The old man said, "Ducks are more beautiful than dots."

I said, "You hunt the duck ever?"

"No hunting," the old man said. "No killing on this ranch, except what is necessary."

Johnny said, "The fish die, don't they?"

The old man said, "Tell me about your surfboarding. I've seen them, going down the coast by Malibu. It looks very beautiful."

"We used to go there a lot before the war. Malibu and

36

Point San Onofre, those are the best places. You can ride them a long way. Sometimes a bunch of us would make up a night party if there was a good moon and no fog. Go to Malibu in our jalopies. Then the girls would dig sand pits and light wood while we would go out on the boards at low tide and dive for the abalones. Then we would ride a wave in all the way with the boards loaded with abalone, and the girls would cook them and someone would have a guitar and there would be lots of beer. Best way of eating there is. Then afterwards we would ride the waves all night sometimes. Come back with the sun."

They were all listening. I wondered why I had been telling them all that. It was the old man. He drew things out somehow.

Johnny said, "What about the girls — didn't they ride the waves too?"

Liza laughed shortly.

"Trust Johnny," she said.

I said, "You can't get two on a surfboard. I did take a dog once."

Liza said, "That wouldn't be much use to Johnny."

"Couldn't take a horse either," Johnny said.

The old man clapped his hands softly together.

"What's the matter, you two?" He turned back to me. "It sounds most fun, to have been young in Santa Monica."

"Didn't any of the girls have their own boards?" Johnny asked.

I thought of Alice.

"Couple did. But they're too heavy and dangerous for most. You can get hurt with those things, have to know what you're doing."

Liza said, "Did you ever get hurt?"

"I was knocked out once. If the front end goes under,

you have to jump sideways fast, otherwise it ups and hits you from behind. I didn't clear."

"What happened?"

"Friend of mine dived for me. I was unconscious."

I remembered Tim Hornbeck, and Alice's face bending close over mine as I came to. The smell of the embers, Alice's wet eyes, the way she covered up and turned back to Tim directly she saw I was all right. Alice and Tim. It had to be Tim who rescued me. Alice and Tim. Bunch of kids we were then.

Liza was saying, "What happened then?"

"He drowned," Johnny said.

Suddenly she turned on him.

"Why don't you get lost?"

"Good idea," he said. "Maybe I'll go to Africa."

There was a sudden silence. The old man's face set firm. Liza burst into tears. She got up and ran into the kitchen. The old man's fist came down hard on the table.

"You get right in there and apologize for that, Johnny."

Johnny shrugged.

"Shouldn't have said that, I guess."

He got up and walked into the kitchen.

The old man and I were left alone. I could see he was very shaken, but all he said was, "At least they permitted us to finish our chicken. Some more wine, Mr. Freeman?"

He had the wine bottle in his hand and he started to pour himself a little wine while he awaited my reply. He had not had any wine before. His hand was shaking a little as he poured the wine.

"Thanks," I said. He passed the bottle and I poured some wine into my glass and said, "Tell me, Mr. Oakes, did Liza lose a boy friend in Africa someplace?"

He took a sip of his wine. Then he took another sip. He put the glass down slowly on the table, twisted the

38

stem a little and looked into the wine in the revolving glass, and then he said, "You remember the *Georges Phillipar?*"

"The French liner that caught fire in the Red Sea, wasn't it?"

He nodded.

"Her father and mother and brother were on a world cruise. They disappeared. He was a Virginia horse breeder. Liza was four. She had no one left. When I read of this in the papers, I persuaded Maria, my wife, that we adopt Liza. I will tell you why." He paused to look toward the kitchen door. It was closed. You could hear voices coming from the other side. They were talking low now, and the tone sounded as though it was quite a drawn-out discussion.

The old man went on.

"You see, Sam, they were last seen safe and alive in a small boat, drifting toward the Abyssinian coast. Now, it's quite possible it sank and they were all drowned. On the other hand it is also possible that they were captured by the Abyssinians. Does that mean anything to you?"

"It does to you?"

He said, "When I was a boy, I once went to the mountains near Turkestan. I saw a slave caravan there arriving from Arabia. I always remember that slave caravan. Some of the slaves were white. Don't think it doesn't still go on today, Mr. Freeman — Arab dhows ply the Red Sea at night, bringing slaves from Abyssinia, mostly dark-skinned, but sometimes, after a shipwreck perhaps, there are white slaves among them. These often bring high prices and much prestige in the eastern Caucasus."

"Does she know of this possibility?"

"Yes. Johnny ferreted it out somehow and told her when

they were children. I thrashed him, but it did no good."
He took up his glass again and drained it and put it down.
"You see, he has always been jealous of the fact that we
adopted her. While my wife lived she could control it
well. Indeed, sometimes they seemed very fond of each
other. Recently I had even hoped that he had forgotten
his jealousy completely. But there, it flares up again worse
than ever before. I do not know what to do, my boy, to
speak frankly. I shall not last much longer. But perhaps
that will be for the best. Then she will not feel tied to
me."

I was thinking what to say. It was not the usual self-
pity of old age. He was truly thinking of Liza.

Outside, a car started up. It was the truck. I recognized
the sound of the motor. It circled the driveway and faded
down the hill.

Liza came in from the kitchen. She was carrying a dish
and looking as though nothing had happened. She set the
dish down on the table.

"Banana custard, Dad, your favorite," she said.

The old man said, "Where's Johnny gone?"

She shrugged. "How should I know?"

The old man grunted.

"Svenson's, I suppose," he said.

I said, "He got the tank this afternoon."

The old man said, "He got the tank, yes. Now he's gone
for the daughter."

Liza said, "Oh, no, Dad. That was last month. You're
way out of date."

"Who is it now?"

"How should I know? He just said he would be back
early so as to be up for the dip in the morning." She
turned to me, gave me a plate of dessert. "Johnny said you
were staying over for the dip. He asked me to give you

a pair of his pajamas and his apologies for hurrying away."

I said, "He's quite a character, isn't he? I never said I would stay the night. I've got to get that car back to old Andresen anyway."

The old man said, "I'm sure Liza can reach him on the telephone. That is, if you would like to stay?" he asked. There was something in his eyes and in the tone of his voice.

I said, "Well, just how many sheep will I have to dip in the morning?"

He laughed. You could see the pleasure in his eyes. He did not try to hide it. Liza looked pleased too I thought.

The old man said, "We only have eighty odd. Just a handful."

"Ninety-three, Dad, please," Liza said. "Will you have some more custard, Sam?"

"No, thank you. And I'll need some jeans too."

"There are plenty of those around. You can't get out of it now. You're committed. I'll go telephone Mr. Andresen."

I watched her walk out of the room, her skirt swinging from her hips. The old man said, "Now I can show you my collection. Come with me."

I followed him. He took me through his bedroom to his study. It was a cozy room, quite small, and very homelike. Cozy is a strange word to use I guess, but it sprang to my mind as I went in. There was a desk with account books open all over it, and in the corner was a stuffed leather armchair under a reading lamp. On the walls there were pictures of snow mountains and forests and the shores of a foreign sea. The old man went to a cabinet standing in the corner, and opened out a long wide drawer. He carried the whole drawer to the desk and laid it down on top of the account books.

"There," he said. "What do you think?"

Stuck into the cork bottom were hundreds of miniature little men. They were about an inch and a half high, not more. Every one of them was in some kind of uniform and each was different. They had been painted with great care and precision and you could tell at once, even without a magnifying glass, that the details of each one's uniform were correct.

The old man said, "When I came to this country I knew no English. In order to learn I read a lot. In order to be interested in reading I studied military history. In order to remember it I began making these soldiers. Then I got interested in the soldiers and read more and more in order to get them accurate. So now I have a collection of soldiers, a knowledge of English, and I have never been to war." He laughed gaily and pulled out a little soldier and handed it to me with a big magnifying glass he took up from the desk. "Here is a soldier of Agincourt. I challenge you to find anything wrong with him."

I looked through the glass and saw how beautifully he had made it. I put it back in the cork, put down the glass, and looked at him and said, "This collection must be very valuable."

He laughed again.

"It probably is. There are few of its kind in the world, I think."

Liza came in as he was putting the drawer back in the cabinet.

He was saying, "It is not that I admire soldiers as such. The reverse. It all came about through my dislike of war. So I decided to study it in order to find out how it could be stopped. But the more I studied the less likely it seemed to me that it could ever be stopped. So then I made all these men in uniform, these soldiers. All have different uniforms, all fought on different sides at different times. But there is one thing you have not noticed about them, Sam."

There was a silence in the little room. Liza was standing quietly as though she knew what it was all about and was waiting for it to be over.

"What was that, sir?"

He beckoned to me to come, and I went and looked at them all once more in the drawer as he was about to close it.

"Take the glass," he said. "Study them closely."

I swept the glass over the forest of little men, each one standing on his spiked feet embedded in the cork. The whole of the panorama of the time of men on earth seemed to pass before my eyes. The sounds of the bugles and the trumpets and the drums and the pipes and the clash of shields and the twanging of bows and the whooshing of great flights of arrows were in my ears, as I studied carefully all these soldiers.

I turned to him and said, "It is indeed a wonderful thing that you have done. But what is there about them that I have missed?"

He chuckled.

"He has missed it, Lizakin. He has missed it. Look. Look again. Look at their faces. What do you see? Can you not see?"

I could hear him chuckling as I was looking through the glass at the faces of all the soldiers and saw that he had made every one of them with an identical face and expression. All the soldiers were the same man.

It gave me a strange feeling. I put down the glass, and he shut the drawer and said, "Give a man a uniform and you take away his face."

Liza said, "It's getting late, Dad, if you want to be up early."

The old man looked up at her from out of his reverie.

"That's right, Lizakin, that's right. Did you talk with Andresen?"

"He said it was all right to keep the car."

"Then will you show Sam the guest house?"

He turned to me and held out his hand with a simple but courteous gesture.

"I will bid you good night and a deep sleep."

I shook hands.

"Thank you, sir, and the same to you."

He showed me out, and Liza shut the door behind her and said, "If you will wait one moment I will get you a pair of Johnny's pajamas."

She went into Johnny's room and came back almost at once with a pair of red and white striped pajamas and gave them to me and said, "I hope these fit. Although Johnny doesn't look as big as you he is deceptively built."

I stretched the jacket across my shoulders.

"Yes, he's deceptive all right."

She looked at me and our eyes held a moment, and she looked away and said, "We'll go out through the dining room and then you can see what there is of the garden on the way."

"Fine."

We walked along through the dining room.

"Just a moment," she said, "and I will get a coat."

She slipped through a door leading off the dining room, leaving it ajar. I could see a bed and a dressing table and walls of a soft blue that looked restful in the shaded light glowing softly on them from the bed table.

She came out again wearing a light coat and smiled.

"It's not cold but I always like to put on a coat when I go out, if I'm not going on a chore. It makes me seem more like a lady and less like a farmer."

"Sounds pretty snobbish to me. Besides aren't I a chore? Extra hand for the dip?"

She tapped me lightly on the cheek as we went out into the patio.

The patio was small and formal. There was a bricked-in barbecue, a large round table with an umbrella.

"This is where we sit and have coffee in the middle of the morning and discuss the price of turkeys or sheep or cattle or hay or how to get the sowing done in time."

"Or the plowing."

"Or the harvesting. Everything in farming seems a race against time."

"Everything is," I said. "Not just in farming."

She did not answer. We were walking through the little patio arch into the garden proper and the moonlight made her face pale. But the light was broken up by the many branches and leaves of a great oak in the middle of the lawn so that it was difficult to be sure about her expression. The garden was quiet at this time of the early night save for the sound of a tree frog. The path led across the lawn under the big tree to a wicket gate in the fence, and then on across the vegetable patch to the guest house. I walked along beside Liza and thought of all that the old man had told me about her.

She said, "Did Dad explain anything about Africa at dinner?"

"Yes, he told me."

She unlocked the side door of the guest house and turned on a light. We went through a little kitchen into a dining room, and then through a bedroom to a long living room, which had a balcony at one end that had a drop stairway leading up to it and a bed on the balcony.

"Quite a place," I said. "Who sleeps up there?"

"Once we had a foreman who was used to sleeping in an old hayloft and he asked if he could build it like that, so we let him."

The walls of the long room were covered with pictures. They were oil paintings of the Santa Serena valley country. You could tell at once they were of the valley because of the red barns and the rolling fields and the sharp little hills making that characteristic jagged horizon. And there were many of a mountain lake. What had been done with the water was uncanny. It was water itself, wet and shining and deep. The wind moved it, so that you could hear the ripples in the still mountain silence surrounding the lake.

I said, "These are your paintings of course."

She said, "Do you like them?"

"Liza, they are wonderful. There is a strange intensity about them. I can't describe it." I thought a moment, trying to put into words what I felt. "Almost a passionate longing, a hunger of love for your home."

She looked at me sharply. Then she said in a low voice, "It's the only home I've got."

There was an intensity in her tone, the same intensity that was in the paintings. Suddenly I had the key.

I said, "It's your adopted home, so you love it the more determinedly."

She turned away suddenly and went and sat down on the divan and took out a cigarette. Her face was taut. I could have bitten my tongue out. I sat down beside her on the divan and lit her cigarette and one for myself, and waited.

She said, "Did Dad tell you why he adopted me?"

That was a tough one. I could not hesitate. It was either lie or say Yes.

I said, "He said your folks were lost off the ship. Can you remember them?"

"I can remember my father and my mother, but not my brother very well. He was away at school a lot and I was just a kid. You didn't answer my question."

She was all charged up.

I let her have it.

"All right he did. He thought they might have been caught and sold into slavery. So what if they were? Do you know how many slaves there are in the world right now?"

She slapped my face.

I sat quite still, watching her. Suddenly she burst into tears. I put my arm round her and soothed her. She stopped crying and said, "I hadn't thought of it like that before. How many are there?"

"Millions and millions. We all may be one day, especially if we don't set them free."

She said, "You feel that very strongly, don't you, Sam? You get all tensed up about it."

"Coming from you, that's a good one."

She nodded slowly, her eyes far away now. She said, "I know. You see I've felt that way ever since the day Johnny told me when I was quite little. And you know what?"

"What?"

"I've always had the feeling, ever since then, that I ought to be one too if they are. It seems wrong for me not to be. Can you understand that?"

"With Johnny around I can understand anything. I'll bet he makes you feel that way."

She went rigid again. She said, "Light me another cigarette, will you? I spoiled this one."

I lit one for her.

"Why isn't he in the war anyway?"

"He got kicked by Black Mark once, damaged a kidney. Let's not talk about Johnny. I wanted to ask you what you thought about Dad."

"I think he's one of the best I ever met."

"I didn't mean that. I'm so worried about him, Sam. Did he say anything to you about his health?"

"Good heavens, Liza, what's the matter with you? He's getting on and maybe he won't live forever, but we all have to go some time. Why are you so worried about everything?"

"It's because he worries about me, about what I'll do when he's dead. And that's bad for him, to worry. The doctor told me so."

"You go round in a circle, don't you, poor kid. You stay to look after him when you know you should leave and find a man. And you know he worries because he's keeping you tied to him. So why not just up and get?"

"And leave him alone with Johnny?"

She put out her cigarette, and as she leaned forward the light from the table lamp fell on her cheek, and for an instant I got the fleeting impression that she was very old, the way the light and the shadow from the lamp fell across her face. Then she sat up and it was gone at once and she looked young again. She said, "Now it's your turn to go through the mill. Why don't you have a girl?"

"Who said I didn't?"

It threw her, either the way I said it or what I said. I could tell it threw her because the color started rising in her cheeks, and as I looked it flooded down over her throat too.

Suddenly I got mad. I said, "So Johnny told you in the kitchen I told him I wasn't married. That it?"

Now we were both mad. Her eyes were sparks of blue.

She said, "I already slapped your face once. How conceited can you get?"

"Plenty, where dames are concerned."

"They throw themselves all over you, don't they?"

"When I get time."

"Like this?"

"Like what?"

"Like this."

It was strange. Her lips were hard on mine. I was kissing her as hard as she was kissing me, but it was strange. It was what she said about a girl maybe, reminding me of Alice. I don't know what it was, but with us right then, even though we were so close, it wasn't right.

And then she felt it too. Maybe she had all along, in a way. It's hard to say. But she let her lips linger a moment; then she kept her arms around me and put her cheek against mine and stayed very still and nobody spoke. I still couldn't be quite sure what she was feeling until she said something, and I waited.

That scent was strong now and sharp as we sat there on the divan, and I could see the picture on the opposite wall across the room where the lamplight just caught it, a painting of the lake. It was the finest of them all, of a still and clear fall day, with the mountains inverted in their water reflection and the thin stream falling through the rocks into the lake.

She said, "What's her name?"

"Who, Liza?"

She leaned back on the divan and looked at me, a woman, not a girl.

"You don't have to be polite, honey."

"I like you, Liza."

"And I like you, Sam. Now we've got that straight, tell me what went wrong with you and her."

"Mind reader yet?"

"Not too hard. You've got a girl, you're not with her, you're all confused up. From the moment I see you, you are. Tell Momma."

I said, "I believe I will at that. You see, when we were kids in Santa Monica we grew up together, Tim Hornbeck, Alice, that's her name, Alice, and I. Most of the time it was Alice and I, but sometimes it was Alice and Tim. When we left for the war it was Alice and Tim, or else I just thought it was. Maybe I was too proud or something. Anyway, Tim got killed, when he was with me. All along we had each had letters from her of course, and Tim and I would talk about her a little, but guarded, Tim acting as though she was for him, and I wondering if that was what she really wanted or not. I could have sworn he was wrong, that she really wanted me, but I wasn't sure on account of the way things were when we left for the war. It's just a lot of silly complicated kid stuff, you know how it would be. Well, when I got back I saw her and told her about Tim. She had already heard he was killed actually, but I wanted to tell her whatever she wanted to know. And now it looks like it was really me, as far as she was concerned, all the time. But I'm still not sure whether that's true or not. Maybe now the fact that he's dead and was my buddy makes it hard for me to accept it without some proof, like taking advantage when his back's turned. It sounds kind of silly, perhaps, all this, but it's been too fresh for me to work it out yet. That's about it, I guess."

She had been watching me all the time I was speaking, and now she sat for a moment turning her necklace around in her fingers.

50

She said, "If I ask two questions will you promise not to blow up?"

"Shoot."

"Was Tim inclined to be a show-off?"

"Well. Isn't any high-spirited kid?"

"I'll take that as affirmative. Question two. Is Alice honest?"

"Double affirmative. That's why I puzzle."

"About her and Tim?" She laughed suddenly, unexpectedly. "Sam Freeman, you're a dope. A woman is honest, but she's still a woman. What else could Alice do? I'll take a bet you were too considerate. Afraid of your own power. I've seen it in you in this short time. You bent over backwards, I'll bet, to let her make up her own mind. That's about the most insulting thing you can do to a woman."

"You really think that's it?"

"Of course that's it." She got up. "I must go, it's getting late."

Now she was poised, mature beyond her years. In that short space of time since we had been sitting on the divan together, she seemed to have become transformed. Maybe, I thought, because those depths had been hidden from me up till now. I got up and went with her to the door. Suddenly in the moonlight her face became a girl's again, framed in her dark brown hair that glinted all over as she raised her face to mine and kissed me lightly as a child.

"Good-by, Sam dear," she whispered softly, "and give Alice my love."

And then she turned and was walking away before I could say any words. I called after her, "Good night, Liza, see you in the morning." But by then she was walking swiftly down the path, and I could not be sure whether she had heard my low voice or not, for she did not answer.

3

I went back into the little house, closed the door and stood for a moment alone in the bedroom, looking at the two beds and wondering which one to take. I picked one at random and undressed and got into bed and almost immediately I started falling asleep with a feeling of calm that was unusual. Just as I was falling asleep I heard Liza's voice in my ears again saying good night and realized that she had said good-by instead of good night, and as I was wondering about this I must have fallen asleep. For the next thing I remember was the neighing of Black Mark.

Even in my sleep, while I still thought I was dreaming, as perhaps I was, I never doubted for a moment that that neigh could belong to any other horse than Black Mark. For the rest of the animals were shut up in their boxes, only the stud himself being permitted to roam throughout the night, and this sound came from out of doors, loud and shrill and continuous, interspersed with much snorting and the stomping of his hoofs.

I got out of bed and went to the window and drew the curtain. The moon was very low now, almost gone, but it was still shedding its light so that you could see the stud's corral quite clearly.

The big black stallion was standing there in the middle of the corral, rearing up and down on his hind legs almost without ceasing, sometimes stopping for a moment to snort and toss his head. When he did this he would walk forward and bend down his head and nudge something that was lying there on the ground. Then he would back away again and start rearing and bringing his forelegs down on the ground at some distance from the place where Liza was lying. She was wearing a white nightdress and I could tell at once that it was she because of the long brown hair which, even at that distance, was shining in the moonlight.

I ran out of the door. The corral fence was some fifty yards. Halfway across I realized I had no stick, no stones, no carrots. I kept on running and thinking at the same time, looking around for something. I saw a man running from the house to the corral. It was Johnny. The stallion saw him too and started toward the fence at full gallop. I thought now was my chance. She was lying about halfway up the corral, right in the middle, maybe some thirty paces from the fence. I thought there was a chance I could get to her and get back over while Mark was distracted by Johnny. But it didn't go like that, not at all. Johnny came running on a diagonal toward me so we both hit the fence at the same time and the same place, and there was Black Mark on the other side coming full gallop. He slid to a stop and reared up, his teeth showing. Johnny put a hand on my arm.

"Keep back."

His hand on my arm was shaky as could be. His face was dead white. He was plain crazed with fear.

"What happened?" he asked. "Did you quarrel?"

I stared at him in a mixture of plain disgust and amazement.

"Why didn't you stay where you were? I could have got in and back."

53

"You couldn't, not with him. I knew this would happen some day. I told her. I told her."

"Listen! I'm going in. You lead him up the fence, try and keep him there while I go."

"It won't work. He'll kill you."

"Run. Up the fence. Go now."

He hesitated some more. Then he turned and ran along beside the fence. Black Mark started after him, reaching out with his head stretched way over the fence, reaching for Johnny with his teeth as he ran. Johnny kept away, just far enough from the fence, kept on running.

I jumped the fence, started running toward her, running light as I could so the stud wouldn't hear me, running like an Indian runs.

I reached her and bent down over her. There was blood in her hair. I felt for her pulse. It was beating. I picked her up in my arms, a dead weight.

I heard Johnny scream, the hoofs pounding.

"Look out, here he comes. Run."

I looked over my shoulder. He was coming full gallop. I stood quite still with her in my arms and turned and faced him. There was nothing else to do.

I believe the thing about fear is timing. Many feel it at the time. Some feel it a little later. If I had still been running away I might have felt it. But right then, as I stood still with her in my arms, I was able to get steady within, just in the moment that he came up toward me.

I called out to him, keeping my voice steady too, but very definite.

"Whoa there, Mark, steady, boy, steady. Whoa."

He stopped. He came right up to within a yard of me and somehow he stopped. It was like she said. Inside the corral he was all right. Yet he had kicked her. I wondered what to do next. The sweat was streaming white in great

54

rivulets all over his black body, and he was trembling all over. Maybe it was because I had her that he stopped. Maybe it was a combination of everything.

Behind him I saw Johnny running. He was running away, back to the house. I wanted to call to him but I didn't dare. The stud was beginning to paw at the ground with his front foot. I didn't like that. I made a swift decision. I pretended to ignore him completely and turned and started walking slowly toward the fence. He stopped pawing and stood quite still. I walked on. After a moment he gave a great neigh. Then he began to trot after me, snorting. I did not turn my head. It took everything I had not to turn my head. I spoke to him.

"There's a boy. There's a boy. We'll soon get her back safe, won't we boy?"

Suddenly he started to prance around. He went all round me in a circle as I walked, kicking up his heels and tossing his head, but never coming really close. It dawned on me then he was putting on a show. An escort show. He was just a great big ham and he loved her and he knew she should be carried in. He loved her.

I got nearer to the fence. Now he stopped his prancing around and came close up, real close. Then he just walked along a pace behind me. I could see out of the corner of my eye he was tossing his head and I could hear him giving little low kind of nickering sounds.

I got to the fence. Now was the tricky part. I didn't know what he would do once I got her halfway over the fence. Maybe he wouldn't want her to go outside the corral, nor me either. You just couldn't tell without trying.

I started to climb the fence. With Liza in my arms it was quite a deal. I got her so that I could lever myself with one arm for a moment, up on the first bar. Then I lifted her so that she was sitting on the top. The stud

55

did not move. He was watching all the time as if he was fascinated. Then, as I got my other foot up and was nearly ready to get over the top, he started pawing again with one foot. I don't know much about horses, but I know that pawing means restlessness. I stayed quite still, in that position, right where I was, one foot on the second rail, one foot on the bottom one, holding her sitting on the top, if you could call it sitting.

I spoke to him, gently.

"There's a boy, Mark. We're going to make it, aren't we, Mark?"

He went right on pawing. I heaved myself up all in one movement and jumped with her. I landed on one knee but I managed not to let her touch the ground. The stud stood still. He had stopped pawing even. It was what he wanted after all. I got up and began walking away. It was then that the shot came.

I turned to look. Black Mark fell with a crash. There was no doubt for a moment. He was stone dead. I looked toward the other fence. Johnny was standing there with a gun aimed on the fence. He must have taken very careful and very accurate aim. And it had been quite unnecessary.

He came running over to me, carrying the gun.

"Is she dead?"

I realized then that when he shot Black Mark he couldn't have known she was not dead. Maybe I might have shot the horse too. Maybe . . .

I said, "No. I'll take her to her room. You get a doctor, quick. Tell him it's a head injury, I don't know how bad."

He took one look at her in my arms. His face was quite white.

"Okay. I'll go telephone. Take her through the dining room door, it's quickest. I'll leave the door open for you."

56

He ran to the house. I followed as fast as I could. I got her into her room and into bed and had covered her up by the time he came back.

He said, "It's a new doctor. He doesn't know the way. I'm going to meet him at the village intersection. He said keep her warm and quiet till he comes."

"All right."

The room was very still when he had gone. I sat by the bed and listened to Johnny's truck fading down the hill. The wound in Liza's head was not bleeding any more. She was lying still. I adjusted the bedside lamp so that the light fell off her face. I parted her hair and looked at the wound. The blood was congealed and I could not tell very much, except that it did not seem to be deep. But even that, I knew, might be serious.

There was a gash about three inches long across her head, but, so far as I could tell without touching it, the wound appeared to be a surface one such as would have been made by a glancing blow that must almost have missed her altogether. I thought Black Mark had probably done it accidentally. From what I had seen he obviously did not want to harm her. Indeed his manifestations had been those of alarm about her being hurt. He loved her.

I sat down again beside the bed. Her breathing was regular. I felt her pulse again and it was going at the same rate as before and quite steady. I wondered what she had been doing, going to Mark like that in the middle of the night. Maybe she could not sleep and felt lonely. She had reason to feel lonely. I felt badly about the way things had gone between us, but it was something unavoidable. I thought about what she had said about her and Johnny, how she was with him. It was a strange relationship they had together. There was that hatred between them, but it was not a simple hatred, somehow.

I heard footsteps coming along the corridor. It was the old man. He was coming across the dining room now. I got up and went to meet him. He looked very surprised to see me. I realized that I was wearing Johnny's pajamas and it must have seemed odd. I put my finger to my lips. I did not wish to startle him, but on the other hand I knew she should not be disturbed with any sudden sounds.

I spoke in a low voice.

"Liza had an accident. But I think she's going to be all right. Johnny's gone for a doctor."

He came up to me rapidly.

"What happened?"

"I don't know exactly. I was asleep over in the guest house and I heard Black Mark. I saw Liza lying unconscious in his corral. I ran and got her. There's a slight wound on her head and she's unconscious, but I think she's going to be all right. Her pulse and her breathing are good. I put her in bed. The doctor said to keep her warm and quiet till he comes."

He gave a little moan. It was a heart-rending sound, although a slight one. He pushed past me and went into her room and stood looking silently down upon her as she lay still in the bed. He put his hand down and gently touched her temple and stroked it with his finger tips. He turned back to me with a bewildered look in his face.

"Such a thing," he whispered. "She must have felt lonely. Sometimes when she was a child she would go out to the horses when she felt lonely. And of late she has been strange." He turned back to the bed. "Lizakin, Lizakin," he whispered.

I said, "The doctor will be here soon. Don't worry now."

She stirred a little. She brought her hand out from under the blankets and raised it toward her head. She

58

was still unconscious. I took her wrist and held it so that she could not touch her head.

I told the old man, "Take her wrist. I will get a towel."

He did as I told him and I went into the bathroom, found a towel and moistened it and came back and placed it over the wound, tying it under her chin so that she could not touch the wound. Her lips moved slightly, but you couldn't hear anything. Then she was still again.

Outside I heard the sound of the truck coming up the hill. Then another automobile. We waited. The old man was still holding her wrist.

They came in. Johnny was still very white in the face. He looked at her and then at us.

"How is she?"

"The same," I said. "Maybe she's coming round soon."

"Dr. Linden, my father — Mr. Freeman."

The doctor was a stocky man in his forties, capable looking. He nodded briefly at the old man and me and we made way for him as he came to look at her, putting his bag down on a chair. He bent over her and untied the towel and looked at the wound. Then he felt around her head with his hands. He had gentle hands. Then he raised her left eyelid. When he had looked at her eye, he took her pulse. She lay still.

He said, "There is no fracture. I will have to stitch this." He looked at me. "Did the horse kick her anywhere else?"

"I don't think so, Doctor, as far as I know."

He grunted, began taking things out of his bag.

"If you gentlemen will wait in the other room?"

The old man said, "Will she have much pain, Doctor?"

"She will have a headache. Concussion headache. She should be round soon. Don't worry, Mr. Oakes, I will take care of her."

The three of us went out of the door and closed it. We went through the dining room into the living room. The old man went to his chair and sat down. I sat on the divan opposite the fireplace. Johnny put a match to the fire and turned on the gas rod below the logs. The three of us watched the flames licking round the logs. Johnny started to pace up and down. The old man took a canister from the shelf by his chair and opened it and took out a cookie and started to eat it slowly.

Johnny said to me, "I will get you a robe."

He went out of the room.

The old man offered me a cookie.

He said, "To eat is good always, even if only a little nibbling."

I smiled and took a cookie and started to eat it. Johnny came back with a robe and I put it on. He turned down the gas under the fire. Now the logs were burning on their own with only a small aid from the low gas flame beneath them. There was a click from the door of Liza's bedroom. Johnny hurried out. The old man got up and so did I. We followed Johnny into the dining room.

The doctor was standing in the bedroom doorway. His face was impassive.

He said, "Bring some more towels. Quickly."

Johnny's face was quite white again now. He turned and ran. Beside me I could hear the old man catching his breath.

He said, "What is it, Doctor? Has she been badly hurt?"

"She'll be all right. But an ice pack will help if her headache is bad. Do you have one?"

The old man said, "I believe there is one. I think Maria had one in her top drawer. It is long ago. I will see."

His words were hard to hear. He moved through the door, a little uncertainly.

The doctor said, "Go with him. Get him to sit quiet and drink some brandy."

"Okay," I said.

Johnny came with the towels as I went after the old man. The doctor took the towels and shut the door.

I told Johnny, "Get some brandy for your father. I'll go with him."

"Brandy. I'll get three of them. What did Doc say?"

"He said to get an ice pack. We're getting it. You get the brandy. And crush some ice."

I turned and went on after the old man. He was looking in a chest of drawers in the far corner of his bedroom, poking about in the back of a drawer. He pulled out various things, a pile of lace handkerchiefs, some ribbons, a prayer book. I caught a smell of lavender and moth balls. He pulled out a rubber bag with a screw top. It had a black and white check.

He stood looking at it for a moment, as though he had forgotten why he was getting it, remembering the ice bag itself. He looked up and saw me. His eyes were hurt like a wounded deer's.

He said, "Pain. So many nights. 'The ice gets warm, Andrew,' she would say." He broke off, held it out to me. "Here, take it to the doctor."

I said, "Johnny's getting some brandy. You'd best sit by the fire again and we'll have a drink together."

He nodded.

"I'll come. Take it now. I'll come."

He was putting things back in the drawer, holding the prayer book. I turned and took the ice bag to Johnny, who was crushing ice in the kitchen. He had been working very fast. Already there was nearly enough ice to fill the bag. I spooned the crushed ice into the bag while he finished crushing the rest. Even though he was handling the ice sometimes with his fingers I noticed beads of sweat on his forehead as he worked.

While I put in the last lot he poured brandy into three glasses and drank half a glass and refilled it, all while I was finishing and screwing on the cap. I left him to it and took the ice bag to the bedroom door and opened it a chink and said, "Here's the ice bag, Doctor."

I didn't look inside.

The doctor said, "Okay. Put it down right there, please, on the floor."

I put down the bag and closed the door. Johnny was standing right behind me with the three brandy glasses.

"What's going on?"

I said, "How would I know? Why don't you take the brandy to your father?"

"Okay. Take yours before it spills."

I took one of the glasses and we went into the living room again. The old man was back in his chair. He still had the prayer book in his hand. He was looking into the fire.

Johnny said, "Dad, I brought you a little brandy."

He looked up.

"How is she?"

I said, "The doctor says she'll be all right. Drink some brandy."

He took the glass and sipped at it.

"That horse. I was always afraid for her. We must send him away."

Johnny said, "I shot him, Dad."

"So?" He sighed. "She will be unhappy. But it had to be."

There was a silence. I looked at Johnny and he caught my glance and looked away.

The old man said, "The shot. That was what wakened

me. Now I remember. Where are the men? Didn't they get back yet?"

"Their car is by the cottage," Johnny said. "They probably did not hear from there. And after the festival."

There was another silence. Johnny finished his brandy. The old man sat looking into the fire again, his brandy glass in one hand, the prayer book in the other. I lit a cigarette. The grandfather clock in the dining room chimed four times. There was no respite from the tension, chiefly because of Johnny. He was like a cat. More and more he seemed like a cat. He seemed to exude felinity. The old man took another cookie from the jar. He took it as a man in sleep, like some people light a cigarette.

The bedroom door opened, and the doctor's footsteps came across the dining room. This time we all stayed where we were. He came to the doorway, polishing his glasses. He nodded briefly at us all.

"She'll be all right now. I've given her a sedative. She will sleep for some time. The head wound is minor. Most fortunate."

He put his glasses back on and looked at me.

"I'm sorry we lost the baby. But, as you know, it was only a three-month pregnancy, so there's no reason to presume any adverse effects for the future. Meanwhile you'll have to get a nurse in for a couple days or so. I'll do that for you if you wish, unless there is someone your wife specifically wants?"

As he looked at me through his newly polished glasses, awaiting my reply, I noticed that he had left a speck of dust in the upper left-hand corner of the right lens. I wondered how it was that he had not noticed this, and then I thought that perhaps it was so far in the corner that it did not come into his present line of vision at all.

I could hear Johnny breathing as he stood beside me. His breathing was fast like a runner's. He was so close I could have hit him without moving, without looking at him. I sat quite still.

I heard the old man's brandy glass being set down firmly on the wooden arm of his chair. I looked at him. He was staring at Johnny. It was worse than any blow I could have struck Johnny.

Then the old man stood up and turned to the doctor. He was very calm and poised and, outwardly, in control of himself now.

He said, "Mr. Freeman is not my daughter's husband, Doctor. Perhaps you would get a nurse from Santa Barbara?"

"I'm so sorry for the error," the doctor said. "But I can get a nurse closer than that, Mr. Oakes."

The old man was looking at the doctor carefully, summing him up. Then he said, "I should like a word with you, Doctor, if you please."

He turned and started walking toward his study. The doctor looked a little surprised, then followed him. That left me in the room alone with Johnny.

I got up and went into the kitchen and poured myself a brandy from the bottle that Johnny had left by the sink. I could hear Liza's voice in my ears as I drank the brandy. I could hear every littlest tone and inflection of her voice as she was saying to me, sitting there on the divan, 'I've always had the feeling, ever since then, that I ought to be a slave too if they are. It seems wrong for me not to be. Can you understand that?' And I had said, 'With Johnny around I can understand anything. I'll bet he makes you feel that way.' And I remembered how rigid she had gone when I said that. The poor kid must have been in a state bordering on complete desperation.

Three months . . . And then she had sat there listening to me about Alice. . . .

I finished the brandy in the glass and put it down and went back into the living room. Johnny was standing staring out of the window into the black. He did not move as I came in.

He said, "I asked her to marry me when she told me. But she wouldn't."

I lit a cigarette, and put the match into the fire, and thought of the spark in Liza's eyes.

I said, "Taste and guts are a good combination to find in a woman."

He did not answer as he still stood looking out through the darkness, but I saw his hands and shoulders tense a little.

The old man and the doctor came back into the room.

The doctor was saying, "I will sit with her until the nurse comes."

The old man nodded and the doctor went out.

I said, "Did you get a nurse all right?"

"Yes," he said, "she's coming from Santa Barbara, so it will be a while yet."

Johnny was still standing as before.

Now he turned and said, "Dad, I was just telling Sam that I wanted to marry Liza but she wouldn't."

The old man did not answer him. He went and sat down in his chair and he looked suddenly very tired.

He said to me, "Sam, will you please bring me a piece of writing paper from my desk and a pen?"

I brought back the paper and the pen to him and he started to write. Johnny had sat down now. He had re-filled his brandy glass and he was sipping at it slowly, staring into the fire. You could not tell by his face and attitude whether his tension had really gone, as he suggested, or whether it was in fact building up higher than ever.

The old man wrote slowly, taking great pains with each word, concentrating his whole mind on what he was writing. I sat and watched them both and wondered what I should do, whether I should suggest going now or wait until the morning. I decided to wait awhile and see what the old man wanted me to do.

When he had finished writing he read through what he had written, making a few little corrections as he went along. He turned to me.

He said, "It is legal for a will to be handwritten. If handwritten, witnesses are unnecessary. Even so, I prefer witnesses. You shall be one. You have just seen me write and sign this. Read it."

He handed it to me. Johnny didn't move. He just sat drinking his brandy.

I started to read it to myself. "Last Will and Testament of Andrew Oakes," he had written at the top, with curlicues.

The old man said, "Read it aloud."

I read aloud.

I, Andrew Oakes, do hereby revoke my previous will. I hereby leave everything that I own to my adopted daughter, Liza Oakes, nee Liza Donniken. In the event she should die before me, I then bequeath everything that I own to the township of Santa Serena, to be administered by the officers of the Bank of Santa Serena in conjunction with the mayor and council, for the purpose of benefiting the citizens of Santa Serena in whatsoever way the administrators shall see fit.

ANDREW OAKES

I finished reading. Johnny was twisting his brandy glass round and round. Otherwise he made no sign.

66

The old man said, "Witness it, please. Sign your name saying, 'I witness the signature of Andrew Oakes,' then your name and the date."

"Okay," I said. I wrote it down as he told me and signed it and put the date on.

The old man said, "Now ask for Dr. Linden to step in a moment."

Johnny said, "Wait a moment before you do that. I have something to say first."

He had ceased the twisting of his glass in his hand now, but he was still gripping the empty glass in one hand while with the other he was holding tight on to the arm of his chair.

"I've wanted to say this many times, but I never have."

He was looking at the old man now as he was speaking, and I think he had forgotten completely that I was there, so great was the intensity of his emotion. You could see the emotion in his face now, carved on it, through and through those slanting cheekbones, and in the lips and in the nostrils and in the pin-fired eyes.

"Ever since I can remember, you have hated me. And you poisoned Mother against me also. I know this, for when I was little I used to wonder why I was me, and I would listen to you and Mother talking when you did not know. And then I found out about Uncle Grigori."

The old man made a little movement in his chair at this. It was only a slight movement, but I noticed it. I could not tell by his face what he was thinking, for it was coldly concentrated upon hearing Johnny's words, but I got the impression somehow that he was surprised. And he seemed to be paying more attention now as Johnny went on.

"It was one night when I was very little and I awakened sweating because I had seen the goblin's dance. They were dancing round my head and throwing fireballs at me. And I got up and walked and listened at your door and I heard you talking to Mother and you said, 'He has Grigori's blood, Maria, he has Grigori's blood.' And she said, 'But he did not understand he was torturing the cat. He did not understand this was a cruelty he was making.' And you said that of course I must have known this. And neither of you understood the truth. For I had seen the goblins in the cat's eyes and I knew they danced in his head at nights, for I can see into the eyes of cats and I know them. So I swung him to drive them out, the goblins, for it had to be done, even though it pained the cat. But I could not explain all this to you.

"And Mother said it then. I've never forgotten. What she said then. She said maybe you were right, that she had passed on bad blood from her family. And I know that is why you adopted Liza. Because you would have no more children in case they were like Grigori or me. So I found out about him. You would not tell me much. But I got it out of her. It took long, bits here and there, over the years, from you both. And I am proud to be like him."

The old man sat up straight in his chair.

"Proud! To take after a thief and a murderer! A killer of men!"

"He was driven to it! The way he was treated! So then he joined with Seminov and the rest and they drove you out."

He paused and you could see the muscle tense behind his jaw.

He said, "If you had not run away, I, Ivan Reschetnikoff, which is my real name, would be in my real country, where I should have been born. Perhaps, by now, I might even be in the Kremlin itself."

The old man got onto his feet. There was a vein pulsing in his temple.

"With Grigori's influence, I am sure you probably would be."

For a moment I thought Johnny was going to burst. I got up on my feet as he took a couple of steps forward. But he stopped short of his father, so I did not stand between them.

Johnny said, "You have twice discarded me. I do not want your foreign land."

The old man's eyes were a little cloudy now as he looked at Johnny.

He said, "Perhaps I should have done what you said. Perhaps I should have stayed. But then you would never have been born at all, for I would have been killed. But now you have your chance. Now you can go to your own land, where you will not feel foreign, perhaps."

Johnny laughed suddenly.

"I will do better than this," he said. "I do not need to go to it. I will bring it over here and you — all of you —" he included me in a sweep of his arm — "will be driven out."

I took a step forward and grabbed him and gave him a backward push toward the door.

"Just like this," I said. "Just like this."

Liza was standing in the doorway, the doctor right behind her. She came forward and stood between Johnny and me.

"All right, Johnny," she said. "Why not just go?"

Johnny stood looking at her a moment.

He said slowly, "You took the words right out of my mouth."

He turned on his heel and went out of the front door. I wondered how much she had heard. I had an idea she had heard quite a lot. She had a bandage around her head. But she did not look sick. She did not look sick at all.

The doctor pushed past me and I looked round. The old man was slumped down in his chair. His eyes were closed, and he was holding his heart with his right hand while he leaned over on his left arm on the side of the chair. He was moving the fingers of his right hand against his heart.

The doctor felt his pulse. Liza gave a little cry and rushed over and knelt down beside him and put her hands on his face and said, "Daddy, I'm here, Daddy. Lizakin is with you, dear."

Outside I heard the sound of the truck motor start up and drive away. I wondered where he would leave the truck and I wondered if the old man was dying and I wondered if Liza should be out of bed and I wondered what I could do, waiting there for the doctor's next move. It all passed in just a few seconds, but it seemed an eternity.

The doctor looked up at me as though catching my thought and said, "Bring my bag from the other room, please."

I went into Liza's bedroom and got the bag. It was on a chair, still open. I carried it as it was back into the living room. The doctor had rolled up the old man's sleeve. He was looking at Liza now, his eyes open. She was smiling to him and stroking his face and whispering something to him that I could not hear.

The doctor took the bag, ran his hands through it capably and brought out a phial and broke it, then he filled a syringe and gave the old man a shot in the arm. The old man gave a little sigh. The doctor took his pulse again, holding it for a long time.

70

The old man opened his eyes again. They looked firmer now. He looked at Liza and said, "You ought to be in bed, Lizakin."

She smiled at him.

"So should you," she said, "so should you."

He took her hand in his and squeezed it.

"Not any more, my darling," he said softly. He looked at the doctor. "Is it all right for her to stay a little while?" he asked.

The doctor said quietly, "It is all right."

Liza's other hand was clenching and unclenching, clenching and unclenching, behind her back, where the old man could not see it. But I could see it. I could see it very well. Every little movement of it.

Liza said, "Dad, I want you to know something. I loved Johnny. I truly did."

He sat quietly for a moment, as though gathering his strength to speak.

Then he said, "And he destroyed it?"

She nodded. The tears were on her cheeks now. He lifted his hand and wiped them gently with his finger.

"He did it with all us, Lizakin. Even his cat. It is in him."

"You don't blame me, Dad?"

"I do not blame you. I do not blame you."

His eyes rested on her face for a while longer as though drinking their fill of her. Then he looked to where I was standing behind the doctor.

He said, "Come here, Sam."

I went forward close to him and he took my hand and he took Liza's hand and put our hands together, then he said, "Look after her, Sam. She is a good girl."

I said, "I will look after her."

Liza was beginning to sob a little now. The old man's

eyes were glazing over a bit. The doctor brought a cushion and put it behind his head. The old man said, "I will rest awhile now I think."

He closed his eyes and let his head sink against the pillow and relaxed his hand on ours and died.

The doctor had his fingers on the old man's pulse and he took them away now and gently parted our hands. Liza put her arms round the old man's neck and sobbed. The doctor and I took her away, and together we led her out of the room to her bed. Nobody said anything. By the time we got her to the bed she had stopped sobbing and hardly seemed to know what was happening.

The doctor turned the lights down and left me to sit with her. He came back with his syringe filled and gave her a shot in the arm. She was beginning to sleep before he had finished giving the shot.

He said, "You stay with her awhile. The nurse should be here soon. I have a lot of telephoning to do. I'll use the other telephone. She may wake any time. Just keep her calm and call me if anything seems to be going wrong. I don't think anything will."

I nodded to him and sat down in the little chair beside the bed, and he went out of the room and closed the door softly behind him. There was just the bedside lamp left on with the blue shade and the room was quiet and feminine and peaceful. You would not think anything had been happening out of the ordinary, a girl sleeping peacefully in her bedroom, its blue walls and the haven of her dressing table with its little bottles and jars and mirrors and lace, and in the other corner of the room a highboy with framed photographs standing upon it giving the evidence of loved ones somewhere in the world, who might even now be thinking of her while she slept.

I got up out of the chair and walked across to the high-

72

boy and looked at all the photographs. There was one of
the old man and there was one of Maria and there was
another of them together, standing under a big oak tree.
I recognized the tree as the one on the lawn, and they
were standing there together holding hands and laughing
a little shyly, in their best clothes. It must have been a
long time ago, a very long time, because they looked quite
young, and underneath was written in a woman's writing,
The Oakes, a big round handwriting more like a girl's than
a woman's, and yet you could tell it was not a girl's if you
looked at it.

The next picture was one of a man and a woman and a
little girl and a horse and a boy of around sixteen or seventeen. They were all in a stableyard with a colonial-looking
house in the background. Virginia or Kentucky, perhaps.
The girl was about four, I guessed, and even at that age I
could see that it must have been Liza by the smile and
the nose and the set of the eyes. The man was in riding
clothes and the woman wore a summer dress. You could
not see the boy's face very well because he was in a
shadow cast by the horse and he was looking the other
way, half bending down, beckoning to a little black spaniel
between the horse's legs coming toward the group from
the stables.

Behind me I heard Liza move in the bed. I put down
the picture and went over to her. She was lying in the bed
watching me.

She said, "He didn't have to shoot Black Mark, did he,
Sam?"

The question took me by surprise. She saw it.

She said, "He told the doctor he had to shoot him to save
me. But you saved me, didn't you? I thought I remembered your arms, being in your arms —" She put a hand
to her head.

73

I took the ice bag from beside the pillow and placed it against her forehead.

"Don't think about things right now, honey. Wait till you feel better."

She took the ice bag from me and put it down firmly on the bed.

"If you'll just answer my question."

I said, "No, he didn't have to, Liza."

Her eyes were wide now, and deep, staring across the room and beyond it, way way beyond it.

She said, "I'll never see him again as long as I live."

"Try to sleep now, honey."

I don't know if she heard me or not, but after a moment her eyes came back to mine, and she smiled at me and took my hand and said, "You're a good man, Sam. Don't worry about me. I'm not in pain. I don't believe I can ever feel pain any more." She released my hand and said, "Now I've got to make my plans."

I saw that she meant this. I knew I would have felt like that too, first to orientate oneself, then to allow the drug to take effect and go back to sleep. Essentially she was a self-reliant person. It was all the more ironic that a snake like Johnny Oakes could wield such a powerful fascination over her. I thought that perhaps such a thing had only become possible by her having spent the formative years with him as her older brother. Or was it just simply an instance of sex attraction?

She must have been thinking about Johnny, too, because she said, "I should have married Johnny. That would have saved Dad. Do you know why I didn't?"

"You can't marry someone you don't love."

"It was because he went for the Svenson girl. Only two weeks after he knew he had me for keeps. Then he did the same thing to her, and now it's some other. You see, as

74

soon as he's sure of someone, he doesn't need them any more."

"You don't have to tell me, Liza. He's a mess himself, that's why. It's an old story."

She nodded. "And one day he'll come back to me. I do something for him that no one else does. But he's going to be unlucky. I'm going to Africa."

I wondered what she meant for a moment, and then I remembered.

"You still believe that your family may be alive?"

"I'm not sure. I've got to be sure. If I can get to Abyssinia, I can go around and make inquiries."

I looked at her lying there in the bed with the strange light in those blue eyes of her, and I thought of all she had so recently been through, and for an instant I almost disliked her somehow. That she should be capable of such an emotional switch so fast.

But then, as she turned her head to look at me for my reply, I suddenly realized that this was her way of sublimation, that the worst thing she could do would, after all, be to sit around Red Barns and brood about the old man whom she had so dearly loved. In place of him she would put the loved ones she had lost in the first place, with the hope that she might find them yet alive.

I said, "That's quite a tall order, Liza, specially in wartime."

"The hell with the war. I can get anywhere. Colonel Frazier owns the Circle Ranch up toward Happy Valley and he'll do anything for me. He could send me straight to the President, or the King of Abyssinia or anyone. You don't have to think about that."

I couldn't help grinning at her guts.

"That's a load off my mind, then. But when you get there . . . This thing happened fifteen, sixteen years ago.

75

And if slave traders picked them up and sold them to an Arab dhow captain, they won't want to talk even if they remember."

"I've got money now. Not a heck of a lot, but enough. If necessary I could even sell this place, though I don't want to do that."

"Then, suppose you find this did happen and you actually did get on the trail. Where's that going to lead you? Clear across the Middle East to the Caucasus Mountains or Turkestan or some place like that, if he was right. Even without it being wartime that would be impossible. You don't speak any languages do you?"

"Isn't there a route of our supplies going up through there to Russia somewhere?"

I laughed, a short one.

"You think our gallant allies will let you in? They won't even let our men beyond the border, the men who are bringing the supplies."

She lay silent. I saw her bite her lip and her eyes began to fill. I felt like a heel suddenly.

I said, "You tell that Colonel Frazier to get me on the ticket too and I'll fly you any place."

She looked at me. Now the tears were running down her cheeks, but she was smiling.

"You would do that for me, Sam?"

"You bet. We'll start soon as you want. Now go to sleep."

She began drying her eyes, dabbing at them a little with her handkerchief. And then she said, in a kind of casual tone, "What about Alice?"

I said, "Oh, Alice will understand. She'll wait."

Liza's handkerchief was still now.

"I see. You mean because you promised to look after me?"

"Of course. You don't imagine I'd renege on it, do you?"

76

Her eyes closed and she lay quiet. For a moment I thought she had gone to sleep, but then she said, "Forget it, Sam. It wouldn't work out, neither for me nor for you, nor for Alice." She opened her eyes and said, "Not that I give a good god damn about Alice, frankly."

But she did about me. I saw it then, should perhaps have seen it before. I could think of nothing to say except to repeat, "But, Liza, a promise is a promise, don't you see?"

"No, I don't. It was a deathbed promise. And they don't count. You should know that, Sam. It's the worst form of duress there is, because it's based on emotion. And another thing, I don't need or want to be looked after. I'm perfectly capable of taking care of myself. Now I'm going to sleep, and you're going away."

She held out her hands to me.

"Good-by, Sam dear, and give Alice my love and tell her she's a lucky girl from me, will you?"

I took her hands and I said nothing, because I knew there was really nothing to say. Suddenly she pulled me toward her. I bent down and she kissed me on the lips.

"That's the second time we've said good-by," she said. "To hell with you, my dear."

"Good-by, Liza dear. I'll keep in touch."

She did not answer me. I went to the door and was opening it, when she said, "Sam, just one thing."

"Yes?"

"Please don't ever come back. Promise?"

I twisted the doorknob back and forth in my hands, back and forth.

"That's a large order, isn't it? You really want it that way?"

She looked at me steadily.

"That way."

I nodded.

"All right. I'll do this. I'll leave my address with the doctor. And I promise not to come unless you or he send for me. Roger?"

"Roger," she said.

I said, "One thing more then. Can I have something to remember you by?"

"You shouldn't, I suppose, but if you wish it, Sam. What do you want?"

"That picture of the lake, under the lamp, with the mountains reflected in the water, you know the one?"

"Yes, I know the one," she said softly. "It's the best one."

"Do you want to keep it?" I asked. "I was just thinking how we never did get to see the lake together after all."

"No, we never did, did we? All right, Sam dear, you may have it."

"Thank you, Liza. Good-by now."

"Good-by," she said, and that was the last thing I heard her say. I closed the door behind me then and went out and saw the doctor and talked with him and left. And I never went back.

I never went back for ten years. . . .

4

In all that time, I heard not one word about either Johnny or Liza Oakes, except for one letter once from the doctor. They had gone out of my life again as fast as they had come into it. That single night and day remained engraved and isolated in my memory, until at times it seemed almost like a dream.

And then, suddenly one day, in the most unexpected place, I ran into Johnny Oakes again, ten years later, on the beach at Santa Monica.

It happened on the hottest day of the year. There must have been a million people on the beaches besides ourselves. Knowing now what Johnny was up to, this was just the situation that suited his purpose best, for the beaches to be as crowded as possible, thus minimizing the chances of anything unusual being noticed.

It was also a million to one shot against my even seeing him at all in the first place.

And he walked right by us, watching the fishing boat.

Alice and I were keeping an eye on the kids. They were in the water, and the waves were big and mean, curling high and over into themselves because of the rip. We had told the kids to stay close in and they did. Little Janie was squatting in the edge of the surf, and Pete was only a little way out, close enough in to be safe from the undertow. I took my eyes off them for a moment to watch the fishing boat. She was a purse seiner, coming right close in. I figured there must be a sardine shoal there, just beyond the breakers.

And then I caught sight of Johnny, walking along the edge of the surf in his swimming trunks, watching the boat, and my heart pounded back ten years in a single stroke. I recognized him instantly, although I had not seen him stripped before. His face had not changed a bit, and you could see by his body that he had kept himself in good shape.

I nudged Alice and spoke low. He was only fifteen yards away.

"Look, hon, that's Johnny Oakes. There, where my cigarette is pointing."

Her eyes followed the line of my cigarette. She studied him.

She said, "I remember you saying he was like a cat. You were right. Are you going to speak to him?"

"Are you kidding?"

Just then we heard Janie scream. She was pointing her little arm out to sea. It was Pete. He had been swept out. We were both on our feet and running. He was caught in a big one. The biggest of the day. As we ran we saw it take him way way up and then smash him. He could not have caught it worse if he had tried. Even with a grown man that is bad. And Pete is only eight.

I hit the water and yelled to Alice to watch Janie. And then I saw that Johnny Oakes was in ahead of me. He was going for Pete, too. He had been standing right next to Janie when she screamed and he was closer than we were. He went in like a bullet and dived into the surf line at the point where Pete had disappeared. As I reached it, too, I dived after them. When I came up, there was Johnny with Pete in his arms. Pete was squirming around and coughing, and I saw at once that at least he had not broken his neck.

"Are you all right, Pete boy?"

Pete looked at me, still spluttering. Although he looked a bit dazed, there was a light in his eyes.

"Sure I'm okay, Dad. Just banged my head a bit."

Then Johnny recognized me. His eyes started.

"Sam Freeman! Of all things. This your kid?"

"Yeah. Thanks a lot, Johnny. That was real good."

It was too, the way he did it, and I knew I should not have wanted to kick his teeth in, but I still did. Of all people to be under an obligation to.

The water had turned and we were fighting it back to the shore. I helped Johnny with Pete. It was tough keeping our footing against the current, but we made it. The usual crowd started to gather, but when they saw Pete was all right they dispersed again. Alice was waiting with Janie. Johnny put Pete down. He was still coughing up sea water.

Alice said, "Are you all right, son?"

"Sure."

He stopped coughing and said, "I caught a big one, didn't I?"

There was too much pride in his voice, and I figured he had done it deliberately when he saw we weren't looking. I smacked his bottom lightly and said, "That's all for today, son."

He looked hurt.

"But Dad, I couldn't help it. I got caught in the current."

"Janie didn't."

"Janie's a girl. She has to stay closer in."

They started one of their shouting matches then, and Alice said, "All right, you two, how about building a sand castle?"

They saw she meant it and went off up the sand together. That left Johnny and Alice and me.

I had to introduce them.

"Alice, this is Johnny Oakes. My wife."

They shook hands and Alice said, "Thank you so much for what you did, Mr. Oakes. That was very quick of you."

Johnny said, "Glad he came to no harm. He was pretty lucky." He said to me, "I will tell Liza that I ran into you. We were talking about you only the other day."

I stared at him.

"You still see her?"

He smiled, a little strangely, in the way that I remembered.

"Yes, indeed. We were married last year. We're still at Red Barns. Anytime you're in the neighborhood, why don't you both drop in? If you'll excuse me now, I have to catch a quick swim before an appointment."

"Well, thanks again, Johnny," I said.

We all said good-by. Alice and I walked slowly back together toward the children. I was thinking about Liza. I became aware Alice was studying me.

I said, "We'd better help with the sand castle."

She said, "You help. I'm going to swim."

There was a little thing in her voice. I pretended not to notice. The kids were divided on a point of procedure with the sand castle. As usual there were two schools of thought. I tried to divert Pete so as to free Janie for her determined turret.

"Look, Pete, see the fishing boat?"

"What about it, Dad?"

"It's a purse seiner."

"What's that mean?"

"Seine means net and purse refers to the type of net which is drawn together like a purse to trap the fish in it."

"What kind of fish? Do many fish come in that close?"

"Sardines do. Right close in."

"But before when I saw that boat it was coming in from way way out to sea. Why didn't it come straight from the harbor to the sardines?"

Alice was starting to put on her cap. She looked at me as I paused.

"How about that?" she asked.

"Because sometimes sardines are farther out and get driven in by bigger fish who want to eat them," I told Pete.

I turned to Alice.

"Didn't you know that, dear?"

Pete suddenly got bored and went back to Janie, but in peace now. He wasn't listening any more.

Alice said, "No, I didn't know it. Boats never catch sardines far out."

She went on putting on her cap. I lay and watched her. I must have seen her do it hundreds of times, but I still like to watch it. I don't think she does it any differently from hundreds of other women, but, to me, it's something to see, when Alice puts on her cap.

She got up and made a face at me.

"Liza. Poo!"

Then she ran down the sand into the water. She didn't stop at the water's edge, just ran straight in as far as she could, as a wave was coming in, and then made a clean-cut dive under it and all you saw was her bottom and then that was gone too.

I waited for her cap to come up again and for a while it didn't, and I began to tense a little as I always do although she does it every time almost, swimming under the sea just for the hell of it. When she came up she was quite a way out, beyond the breaker line; she lay there on her back and waved at me and I waved back, and she kicked up her legs and turned over and started swimming again, straight toward the fishing boat.

That made me mad. She had no right to fool with that current like that, even if she was still a wonderful swimmer. She makes me a nursemaid and then swims way out to the boat, when it should have been the other way round. I guessed she was doing it deliberately because of Liza's name coming up. I kept a good eye on her. Her overarm was like a machine.

Then I saw another swimmer coming round the boat, coming back in. I had not noticed him going out, but there were so many people and I had not been watching all the time anyway. I watched him to see how he was doing against the current, because that was what Alice would have to be doing when and if she ever decided to return. And he wasn't doing too good.

Partly it was the current, but it only took a few strokes of his for me to see that he just wasn't a real swimmer. I thought the man must be a moron to have tried swimming round the boat. I watched them come toward each other, and then I saw them stop a moment and talk. I couldn't hear what they said across the water, of course, because of the noise of the surf. Then they each went on again as before, Alice toward the boat, he toward the breaker line. I got a sudden impulse to go out to Alice.

I got up and called over to Pete.

"Listen, son, I'm going in the water. Now you stay right here and take care of Janie." I made my voice real fierce. "Stay right here, understand?"

I saw that he registered it.

"Yes, Dad, okay. When you get back may we swim again?"

"If you're good, yes. Don't forget now."

He smiled all over.

84

"I won't."

I ran down the sand into the water. There was a lull in the breakers now as I started swimming out. I thought to myself that it was fortunate for the man coming in. He didn't look the type that would like those breakers. There was the usual line of men waiting to ride the next wave, even if it broke their necks, just as Alice and I had always done up to a few years back.

The swimmer from around the boat was in among them now. Just then I noticed Johnny Oakes right close to me. He had not seen me. He was swimming toward the man coming in. I went on my way. But I had only just turned my head away when I heard Johnny's voice calling out, "Is it Friday today?"

I turned and looked. He was speaking to the man coming in. Considering it was Sunday it seemed a crazy thing to ask a man. The other man looked at him and immediately started swimming toward Johnny. They got together and I couldn't hear what the other man replied. I noticed that Johnny started helping him in after that. I could not figure it out and went on swimming toward the boat.

I could see Alice coming back now. Her white cap was just circling around the stern of the purse seiner. The overarm was going the same rate as ever, even after she had turned into the current. As we closed the gap between us I felt both relieved and also a little sore at the same time. She looked surprised to see me.

"Sam! Are the kids all right?"

"Don't worry about them. I took care of that before I came to watch over you in this kind of ocean. Think you're Chadwick?"

She laughed.

"With some training maybe. Fuddyduddy."

"I'll give you some training."

I swam close and grabbed at her, but she saw me coming and dived sideways. Then she ducked my head. Next time I caught her good, half nelson. We both went under. But when we came up I still had her. I got her over my shoulder then and got in one good spank in the right place before we went under again. I let her go and we both came up spluttering.

"Sam! The kids were probably watching."

"That's right. Probably give Pete an Oedipus complex."

"Hey, we're nearly back to the boat."

We started swimming again. It was quite a current, but it wasn't as bad as it could have been. We swam along together.

After a few strokes she said, "Sam, did you see that man I met?"

"Yes. Why?"

"He must be crazy. I thought he looked in trouble so I stopped and said Hullo. He looked at me and then guess what he said?"

"What?"

"He said, 'Is it Friday today?' So I said, 'No, it's Sunday. Are you sure you're all right?' And then he sort of clammed up and said he was fine and went on his way."

I swam a few strokes.

I asked Alice, "Tell me, did you see that man on his way *out* to the boat?"

She looked surprised.

"No. Why?"

"I heard Johnny say the same thing to him about Friday. It must have been a password. He mistook you for Johnny. You were the first person he met and you spoke to him. Johnny was to meet him off the boat. That boat was acting strange anyway. Suppose it had been out and met a submarine and picked him off it?"

Instinctively we both turned and looked at the boat. It was still there, as though it was fishing.

"Did you see any nets in the water?"

"No. But I didn't look especially. There may have been."

"I think I'll go swim around her. See what I can see. We'll never trace Johnny in that crowd anyway."

She put a hand on my arm.

"Please don't, Sam."

"Why not?"

"There's nothing to see for one thing. And for another you've horsed around enough."

"So, getting too old am I?"

"Look, let's ride this one in."

A big one was coming just right for where we were. We both caught it together and rode it in. It took us right up onto the sand. The kids were standing there. Janie was crying.

"What's the matter, honey?" Alice asked her.

"Pete said you was sinking."

Pete said, "I didn't say sunk. I said sinking for fun. She doesn't understand English. Can I swim now, Dad?"

I remembered that I had promised him. I looked at the boat. It was still there.

"Okay," I told him. "Just two minutes. Then we'll go get ice cream. How's that?"

He ran in the water, shouting loudly, "Strawberry and vanilla, strawBERRY and vanILLA." Then he started swimming in a tight circle.

I watched to see that he didn't drift out. Alice let Janie splash in the surf. The boat was still there. There was no sign of Johnny and his friend. But they could have been any one of a thousand couples. Probably they had gone in a car by now. A lot of people were beginning to leave. Quite a breeze was springing up and the sun was setting over Point Dume. I thought of Johnny and Liza, and dried myself on a towel.

We got the kids out of the water and dried off and collected our things and started walking back to the car. The kids ran ahead and started playing with the window buttons on the convertible.

Alice put her arm in mine. She was wearing a gray skirt over her bathing suit and a white terry cloth top with two big buttons. Snug.

"Remember me?" she said.

I squeezed her arm.

"I've got to check up on that boat, Alice. We'll go to the pier and ask around."

She said, "It's still there, just fishing. Sam, I'm sure it's too fantastic. Why don't we just leave it be?"

"Not get mixed up in something, huh?"

I felt her arm tighten a little in mine.

"Why should you anyway — it isn't as if you've no responsibilities any more."

"At least I should turn in a report."

She didn't answer that. When she didn't like anything she had a way of simply not answering. This time I ignored it. She took her arm out of mine.

We got to the car. The kids were still fooling with the windows so that they were going up and down, up and down, and the reflection of the afterglow of the sunset was going up and down with them. It was very beautiful.

I turned to look at it and Alice turned with me. In October the colors are very beautiful indeed, perhaps not quite so good as they can be in November, but it is always something to see, the October afterglow over the ocean. You could still see Point Dume away on the horizon. And in the foreground, silhouetted sharply against the colored sky, was the fishing boat. It was beginning to move now, making for the pier and the harbor. They had not been fishing very long. It did not look as if they had been fishing there at all. They had stayed just long enough to look as though they had investigated for sardines, in case anyone had been checking them from the pier, maybe.

Beside me I felt Alice give a little shiver through her body. She was standing close to me now, and though she did not say anything, I knew that she was frightened because I was too.

5

We were driving along the bottom road instead of up through the Palisades as we usually did, and I could see the fishing boat in the gaps between the houses, and Pete said from the rear, where he was clambering around with Janie, "Why don't you go up, Dad? Are we going back Olympic?"

I said, "Back along Olympic, Pete boy, not back Olympic."

Janie said, "We're going back along Olympic, back along Olympic, it's got a lady's leg on it, bigger than any lady's leg, bigger than Mamma's leg."

I said, "We're going to the pier to buy sand dabs for dinner, that's where we're going."

Alice was sitting quiet beside me and she gave me a quick glance but she said nothing, and Janie said, "Sand dabs, golly, I like sand dabs, look Pete, I'm a sand dab," and Pete said, "You're not flat enough, but if you want to be one, I'll cut off your head."

I was thinking that they must all be Reds on that boat if I was right. I was trying to work out exactly what to do. We had nothing to go on. I wanted to talk to Alice, but the kids were too sharp and they remembered things and repeated them later. You never knew when they would repeat something. It was like having a couple of mynah birds.

Alice said, "I wish my French was better."

"That's what I was thinking, so perhaps we don't need it."

Pete said, "Why do you want to talk French?"

Alice said, "So I can talk to Frenchmen and learn about their country."

Pete said, "I think it's so I wouldn't understand if you talked French."

Janie said, "Do sand dabs understand French? Do they?"

We turned up the pier ramp and went up it and onto the pier. There was a big moon and there were stars and there were the lights on the pier and all along the coast and bobbing on the sea in little boats. The fishing boat was still only halfway, if that, so we had plenty of time to get to the end of the pier where the lifeguard station was and warn them.

There were still a number of people on the pier, most of them making their way home from fishing. Many were still fishing from the rails. As we were halfway down the pier Janie started to whimper a little and said she had to go. Alice swore under her breath. I stopped the car by a café and told Alice that I would meet her at the end of the pier. I got Pete in front with me and drove to the end and found a parking place and parked. From the rail ahead you could see that the fishing boat was still some way off. I told Pete that he should sit in the car and wait. I said that I might be some time, but that he was to sit in the car and wait and not to move out of it and that later we would go and get the sand dabs. And the ice cream. He didn't like it at all, but he saw that he did not have to give me any trouble just then because of the way I said it. I went into the lifeguards' office and found them both on the telephone.

Soon one of them hung up and came over to me. He was polite and courteous, but you could see that he was busy. Suddenly I felt foolish, very foolish, and I wondered how to begin.

I said, "I want some information. Are you the people to see with regard to inspection of incoming boats?"

He looked at me.

"We're lifeguards. You want the fish and game people — checking licenses you mean?"

"No, checking people."

"I don't get it." He was getting impatient.

I said, "Look, who checks the people coming in?"

"Nobody does. Why should they?"

It didn't make sense.

"Suppose someone was picked off a submarine by a fishing boat last night and brought in to this pier, they could land undetected?"

"That's right, place is wide open." He leaned forward a little. "Don't you remember in the war, how they landed those people from a sub?"

I felt dazed. Outside I could see that the boat was getting close in now. It was pulling around to the landing jetty on the south side of the pier.

I said, "Thanks a lot," and walked out of the office and went over to the car. Pete was bouncing around, ready to explode, like a dog that had almost wagged his tail off. I let him out and said that we would take a walk around on the pier a little before getting the sand dabs if he liked. He walked along a curb and over a bench and started telling me about a friend of his who was designing a rocket ship. He said that his friend was going to be the first man to fly to the moon, but he was having trouble with his landing arrangements.

We reached the crane over the jetty and I said, "Let's

stop here and watch the fishing boat unload, shall we?"

He shrugged and looked at the boat. "That's the same boat that was by our beach. Isn't it, Dad?"

"Looks very like it. Here come your mother and Janie. Go and tell them we're here."

"They can see us under this light. Look at those fish. What kind of fish are they, Dad?"

"What would you say?"

"They're sardines."

There could have been more. Either it was that the fishing had not been very good or they had not been trying long enough. There were four men altogether, just ordinary everyday-looking men, fishermen. They were all behaving quite ordinarily, going about the business of unloading the fish in the normal manner, filling a crate with them, then putting the crate in a net that was hoisted by the crane and then emptied into a truck near us.

Alice and Janie came up, and Janie started to tell Pete about a blue barrel of shells that she had seen and Pete started to tell her about the fishing boat. Alice and I leaned close together over the rail by the crane, and I told her what happened with the lifeguard as we watched them unload. The kids could not hear what I was saying because of the noise of the crane and the shouting between the men in the boat and the man on the crane.

When I told her she said, "So you see you must have been wrong. They wouldn't go to all that trouble if they could land him here. He could just act like one of them and no one would know."

"The man on the crane would know. All kinds of people might know, Alice. They'd be taking an awful chance. I agree it's lax of the authorities in times like these, but still I know if I was one of those Reds I wouldn't risk it, landing a perfect stranger here. You don't realize how everyone knows everyone."

She didn't answer. I looked at the man on the crane. There was a lot of kidding going back and forth and they called him Ed or Eddie and you could see at once that they had known each other a long time. Of course you could not tell anything from that. Maybe they were Reds and he wasn't. Or maybe none of them were. Or maybe they were all plain, old-fashioned smugglers, every man jack of them.

Alice was looking down at the boat. There were several glistening places now on the deck under the lights from the jetty where you could see the fish had been.

She said, "Sam, you know what? They must have caught those sardines earlier. They were probably coming from around Point Dume when we first saw them. They probably had caught them further up the coast, then rounded the Point which is out to sea from where we were, because of the bay coast line."

"And they went to meet the submarine in between. That's it."

"If there was a submarine," she said.

I didn't answer her. They had finished the unloading, and Ed was saying they would never get rich on that and one of them said the run had stopped cold and it was probably Ed's fault for holding such bad thoughts. Two of the men were coming up the steps to the truck while the other two were getting the seiner off to her moorings, towing a dinghy behind them as they left. Janie pulled at Alice's skirt and said, "Peter is being bad," and I looked and there was Pete running down the steps toward the men coming up. It was much too late to stop him.

He met them halfway up the steps and said something that made them laugh. Neither Alice nor I could hear anything except the word sardines, and Janie kept saying, "Oh me-me-me, look at my brother, oh me-me-me," making like a contralto so that we couldn't hear what Pete was saying. Alice told Janie to shut up and by then Pete and the men had reached the top beside us and Pete said, "This is my mother and dad. My mother swam round your boat when you were by our beach. My mother is a very good swimmer indeed."

It surprised them. It was more something that you sensed rather than anything that you saw. There was nothing to see, just the two fishermen standing there in front of us, one a large man of around thirty-five with blue eyes, who made you think of all the clichés about salt ever made. The other one was much smaller and he also had black hair, but his eyes were brown and kind of murky-looking and observant, in an ill-educated sort of way, as he looked at Alice.

They were both looking at Alice and she smiled at them and said, "My husband here said that I may easily have spoiled your fishing by swimming around your boat so I came to apologize."

They went on looking at her and then the big one said, "No, lady, weren't no sardines right there to disturb anyway. We were just trying it out as a last chance, but we saw right away it was no good tonight."

And then the other one said in a slow kind of drawl that could have been Southern yet had with it an Italian inflection which created an odd effect, "You're a powerful swimmer, ma'am. I was watching you. Had best take a care of those currents. Can get into aplenty trouble that way in Pacific."

Ed had come over now from the crane.

I was just saying to the smaller man, "I'm glad you said that. I've been saying that for years, but I'm only her hus-

95

band. Say, we also came over to buy sand dabs — did you catch any sand dabs?"

Ed roared at this, a great gust of laughter, as though it was the cutest thing he had heard since 1946, and he said, "Those guys couldn't even catch enough sardines, mister."

Janie was staring at Ed with round eyes and she said, "My dad's very clever, isn't he? He's as clever as a barrel of funnies, my opinion."

Pete said to Ed, "She means monkeys. Will you show me how to work the crane? I want to work a crane when I'm fifteen."

You couldn't tell whether there was anything or not. You couldn't tell one way or the other.

Salt said to Pete in an aggrieved way, "You said you was going to work a purse seiner just now," and Janie started to tell the brown-eyed one about the barrel of shells and Alice went to collect the kids and Ed came up to me with a lighter for my cigarette, and while I was lighting it he said, "Steve's right, your wife should watch for the riptides — so she swam right around the boat, did she?"

I finished lighting the cigarette.

"Thanks. Yes, she did. But she's a fine swimmer. She can take care of herself."

He swung me by the arm and pointed to the breakwater at the end of the harbor.

"You see that? Right along my arm, there." He took my arm and made me look along his so that I could see where he was pointing.

"The gap near the end you mean, where the rocks are lower?"

"Yeah, that's the place. I saw a woman killed right there, five, six years ago. She was a wonderful swimmer. But

96

that's where we found her. I didn't see her actually killed, you understand, but that's where we found her."

He looked across at the other two and shouted. "You remember finding that stiff —"

I trod on his toe hard.

I said, "The kids." I trod on it harder than I would normally because I didn't like him pawing all over me.

I said, "Well, thanks a lot, we'll be getting on to the fish market. Hope you all have better luck next time."

They said good-by and we all went off, walking down the pier to the fish market. I hoped that we looked what we were, a plain ordinary American family going to buy some fish, with nothing else on our minds but that.

There was quite a crowd in the fish market because it was near to closing time and we had to wait our turn. There were still enough sand dabs left, and they were fresh caught too, so Alice bought them and we all went back to the car.

The truck had gone by then and there was no sign of the men. You couldn't tell for sure which one of the moorings would be their boat because of the number and the moon going behind a cloud bank, and we got in the car and drove home. It looked as though maybe the fog was coming in and the weather was on the turn.

As we drove back along Olympic, I was thinking to myself that maybe it was the last of the good weather for the year and maybe the family would not go on the beach together again until next year, some time in the spring perhaps or the early summer. I thought how it would be next year, if we would all still be together in peace and going to the beach on week ends, or if the other thing would have changed all that. And I knew, driving along with Alice telling the kids a story to keep them from wanting their dinner and feeling glad myself that we were

97

nearly home, that I did not want anything changed ever, as though we could always be this family at this age and driving along this road at this moment for the rest of our lives. And then I ran through an amber light, and there was a motorcycle cop right by it.

The light only just changed as I reached it, but he picked me up just the same and technically he was correct. I think he might not have given me a ticket if I could have found my license. But my wallet was gone. It had been stolen out of my pocket. There had only been a few dollars in it, but whoever had taken it had got all my identification, showing where we lived.

Alice and I did not say anything about it in front of the children except that it must have been taken in the fish market. But I think that she was thinking the same thing as I was. It might have been stolen in the fish market, but the only other person who could have taken it was Ed, the man on the crane.

6

After dinner, when the children had gone to bed, Alice and I did the dishes. I stacked them in the sink ready for her to wash when she came back from saying good night to the kids. I knew that she would not be long because they had almost fallen asleep over the dinner table. Then I opened the kitchen door to let the smell of the fish out and stood in the doorway. The fog had not reached our neighborhood and the moon was still bright. Across the garden you could see the great ragged eucalyptus motionless against the stars and the high wooden fence behind the herbaceous border. There were some toys left lying on the lawn by the swing, and Pete's upturned wheelbarrow exactly as he left it, halfway from the flower bed to the bonfire, the weeds tumbled out onto the grass, when he had heard me driving back from golf, because he knew we were going to the beach.

I walked out across the lawn and picked up the weeds and wheeled them to the bonfire and tidied up the toys. It was still very warm, and as I walked back across the lawn I could hear all the little neighborhood sounds, the Daugherty's garbage lid, a radio playing softly, a roller skate on the sidewalk, and, farther away, a car honking on the main highway. When I got back Alice was at the sink.

I took up a cloth and started to dry the glasses as she washed them.

I said, "I'm going to call the F.B.I." ·

She did not answer for a moment, holding a glass under the tap. There was a little whiteness in her face. She had been going through something, I could tell that.

She said, "Sam, those men. I was thinking about them in there, when I was saying good night to the kids. Pete fell asleep as soon as he hit the pillow, even before Janie. She didn't take much longer. Then I sat on a moment and I thought of those men."

She put the glass down on the draining board and she must have been gripping it for I heard it crack.

"If only we hadn't gone to the pier they couldn't have found out about us."

She was trembling a little. Alice. I put my arms around her.

"I'm sorry, baby. But they won't harm us."

Suddenly she burst into tears.

"They might if you set the F.B.I. on them. They'll guess it was you, and they know where we live from your wallet. Oh, Sam, please don't do any more. Please. Don't you see, if we do nothing they'll do nothing, because they don't know if we suspect them or not."

She was crying all the time she was talking and it all came out in a rush and it didn't make too much sense to me, but I had never seen her scared before, and I could not take that.

"Anything you want. Just quit that shaking or you'll have me doing it, you goat."

She was so surprised that she stopped crying all at once and stared at me with wide eyes. Wide eyes of blue with much water in them.

"Sam! Why haven't I ever tried that before. It really worked."

"Great actress, ain't you. Who are you kidding?" I kissed

her in each eye. "Actresses don't have salt in their tears."

"What do they have, dear?"

She was still trembling a little. I could feel her body still quivering a little against mine.

"Glycerine," I said. "Tastes much better. Let's get the dishes done and get to the crossword."

Now she was calm again. She laughed and bit my ear and turned back to the sink. We finished the dishes together and she swabbed down the sink while I put out the garbage and got the paper from the front lawn so that we could do the crossword. The crossword was in the second half of the paper and I threw down the front portion without even looking at it and opened up the crossword page in the second section.

Alice came in just as I sat on the divan and put the paper on the coffee table so that we could sit together and do the puzzle like we always did. She picked up the front portion of the paper from the floor where I had dropped it and put it on the table and sat down beside me, and I think we must both have seen the headline at the same time. It said, UNIDENTIFIED SUBMARINE SEEN OFF SOUTHERN CAL.

We read it together, the whole thing, sitting on the divan close.

An incoming Constellation had sighted a submarine two hundred seventy-three miles off Point Dume at dawn. The submarine was traveling west northwest, just below the surface, in the act of making a slow dive when seen. The navy said that none of their submarines was in the vicinity. The navy said that when they searched for the submarine, they could not locate it. Search was continuing. You could not tell if the navy was a little skeptical about the report or not. But I knew that they would not

101

find the sub. It had dived for the day, and tonight it was on its way back to Russia.

I was figuring as I read. The fishing boat did about fifteen knots. On the surface, as it would be at night to make time, the sub would do the same. The boat arrived back at Santa Monica around seven in the evening. Dawn was around seven too, daylight time, just after the equinox. Twelve times fifteen was one hundred and eighty miles out to sea at dawn. The submarine was two hundred and seventy. Ninety miles separated them at dawn, each going in the opposite direction at fifteen knots. That meant that the boat and the submarine must have met three hours before dawn to hand Friday over, at four A.M. Why would they wait till four A.M., only just giving the boat time to get back before the swimmers went home?

There was a full moon. That was why. They had had to wait for the moon to set because of the danger of being seen handing Friday over in the moonlight. And the full moon set around three-thirty or thereabouts. It checked.

I told Alice how I had it figured. But I don't think that she took it in too well. I don't think that she even troubled to listen to the figures much. I could see in her face that she knew darned well that it must check.

And then she said, "Well, Sam, I guess this is it. We can't not tell the F.B.I. now. After all, we're Americans."

There was a light in her eyes. I suddenly had a thought flash through my mind as I looked in Alice's eyes then. I bent forward and kissed her and said, "The Kremlin doesn't have a chance."

I found the telephone directory under a pile of papers in the table rack and looked on the first page where it says Federal Bureau of Investigation. MAdison 7241. I picked up the receiver and had already dialed the letters MA when the front door bell rang.

I put down the phone and went to the door and opened it. I was ready for anything, but I was surprised at what I saw. He was well dressed, very neat and unobtrusive, in a business suit, carrying a brief case. He looked like an attorney maybe, young, and in good shape. In very good shape, the way he stood on his feet, the alert in his eyes.

"Mr. Freeman?" he asked.

"What can I do for you?"

"My name is Mason Brown," he said. "George Mason Brown. "I wonder if I could come in for a moment."

"Was it anything very important, Mr. Mason Brown? It's getting late."

He took his wallet out of his pocket and for a moment I thought that he was going to take out a card. But then I saw that it was my wallet. He was watching my face.

He said, "You lost this tonight, didn't you?"

He said "tonight." If it had been picked up he could not have known when it was lost. Only if Ed had told him when it was that he had picked my pocket.

I kept my face as casual as I could. That is, I made it eager and bright, making like a man who had lost his wallet and that was all.

I said, "Why that's wonderful, Mr. Mason Brown. Come right in, do."

I turned to Alice, who was standing in the middle of the living room.

"Darling, this gentleman is Mr. Mason Brown. He has found my wallet. This is my wife, Mr. Mason Brown."

Alice handled it all right. In a sudden thing Alice was all right.

She said, "How do you do, Mr. Mason Brown. Very kind of you to bring it back personally. This calls for a drink. What will you have, Mr. Mason Brown?"

I shut the door.

He laughed easily.

He said, "Nothing, thanks. You haven't asked me how much money is still in it?"

"I think there was a five and two ones."

He held out the wallet with a look of relief.

"I'm glad to say that's the amount in the wallet. My credentials, sir."

I took the credential card. It said, Mr. George Mason Brown, Special Agent, Federal Bureau of Investigation.

I looked at the card and back at him.

"Since when has the F.B.I. started picking pockets?"

"A good question, Mr. Freeman. The man concerned is not a member. He is what you might call an enthusiastic amateur trying to help us."

"You have other identification, Mr. Mason Brown?"

He gave me a quick look. I think he was smiling a little inside. He produced a police badge.

I said, "If it's all right with you, I'll just make quite sure."

I picked up the telephone and dialed the F.B.I. number. A girl answered. I was watching Mason Brown all the time. Alice was watching us both. I could see in her face now that she was beginning to feel that it was all right. There was something about Mason Brown, the way he radiated.

I asked the girl if they had an agent called George Mason Brown, explained he was there now. She had me hold the line. Soon a man answered. I had to tell him all over. He said to put Mason Brown on the line. I gave Mason Brown the telephone.

He said, "Mason Brown here. Ident Aphis."

The other man said something.

Mason Brown said, "Yes. That is correct. Tell Sal from

104

me to take a raise. No, the taxpayer pays it." He laughed, said, "Just a minute," handed me back the phone.

I got on the line and the man said, "We are satisfied if you are, Mr. Freeman."

I said, "Thank you very much," and hung up. "Sit down, Mr. Mason Brown."

We all sat down.

Alice said, "*Aphis*. That was the name of the boat, Sam. I remember now, I saw it when I swam around it."

George Mason Brown tried not to look interested, but he didn't try very hard.

He said, "Did you happen to notice, Mrs. Freeman, if there were any bathers from the boat?"

Alice looked at me now. Her eyes had a quest in them, as though she was searching inside herself.

I kept my face noncommittal. This was something for Alice to decide, I thought.

She saw it and turned back to Mason Brown.

"Tell me, Mr. Mason Brown, you say the man who took the wallet was for you?"

"Yes."

"Then the other men — the men in the boat I mean — they don't know about us? Who we are?"

"No."

She said, "You tell him, Sam. Tell him the whole thing."

I told him. I told him about Johnny Oakes and everything, the whole story. There was a way that Mason Brown had of listening that helped. He made you feel it necessary to be brief and to the point, that he was going right along with you.

When I had done he nodded, went to the telephone and asked someone to run a check through on Johnny Oakes.

He put down the phone and said, "They're checking with Washington now. We'll know in twenty minutes, maybe less. From your story it's likely that he never disclosed himself to anyone else. Pity you never turned his name in."

"I haven't heard of him in ten years."

"I understand." He turned to Alice. "This swimmer. What did he look like?"

"I knew you were going to ask that," she said, "and the trouble is I can't describe him. He had dark hair, I think, and he looked — well, just a nondescript sort of man, the sort of man you don't notice. I only noticed his bad swimming."

"His voice?"

"Well, there again, it was just an ordinary voice."

"Any accent?"

Alice hesitated.

"It was what I suppose you'd call a cultivated accent. Cultivated or cultured, whichever. Just a little too good."

"Good?"

"Well, too English or too Oxfordy or something. Like some Europeans speak English, maybe. But maybe I'm just imagining it afterwards, it was that hard to tell."

He turned to me.

"How would you describe him?"

"I didn't hear him speak, but he looked about as my wife said. There wasn't anything about him. I'd say he was around forty or so, maybe less, maybe more. Average build, from what you could see, dark brown hair or maybe black."

"I don't think it was black, Sam."

"I would have said so, but maybe it was dark brown."

"Round face, long face, big nose, turned up nose?" Mason Brown asked.

I said, "It wasn't either round or long, his face. And his nose, I don't know, it wasn't pronounced or anything. I think he had a big mouth, but maybe that was just because he was breathing hard, getting his breath. Is that what you'd say, Alice?"

"Oh, I definitely don't think he had a big mouth, Sam. Because I remember after I'd answered his question, he sort of shut his lips and I thought it was kind of little."

"Mean, thin-lipped?" Mason Brown asked.

"Well, I didn't notice his lips were thin exactly, but he sort of clammed up suddenly, you know, like a trap. I'm afraid we're not being much help, are we?"

Mason Brown laughed in his easy way. You would think he was playing a friendly game of canasta at the club.

He said, "Maybe more than you think, Mrs. Freeman."

The telephone rang and I said, "That's probably for you."

He nodded and picked up the receiver. He listened for about as long as it takes to say, no soap, and then he said thank you and hung up. From his reaction I figured there was nothing on Oakes.

He sat for a moment thinking of something and Alice and I sat quiet too, waiting to see what he was going to say next. Perhaps we both knew what was coming. I think that Alice knew because of the way she was sitting, her back very straight, and casually smoothing the curl on her forehead.

Mason Brown said, "You say that Oakes invited you to stop in and see him up there?"

Alice said at once, "It was quite casual. He didn't really mean it."

I said nothing. I could see that Alice was going to carry this ball.

Mason Brown said, "Still, if it happened to be your husband's vacation and the family was passing by, and maybe he was showing you the valley, what would be more natural than to take him up on it?"

I waited for Alice. I didn't have to wait long.

She said, "Look, Mr. Mason Brown, we've done our duty. Since when does the F.B.I. ask strangers to do its work? Why, we might be anybody for that matter. How do you know we're not spies ourselves?"

Mason Brown said, his face impassive, "Smithson Arthur Milton Freeman. Born Santa Monica. School Santa Monica High. Police record. Fined twenty-five dollars with one Timothy Hornbeck for disturbing the peace at Twenty-third and Montana, Santa Monica, August 8, 1940. Honorably discharged Army Air Corps September 1943. Purple Heart, Distinguished Flying Cross, Oak Leaf Cluster. At present employed Augustus French, Insurance Agents, Beverly Hills. Married Alice Mounts, also of Santa Monica and with whom he went to school, in December 1943. Two children. Peter and Jane, aged eight and five respectively. I don't think you are required to swear an oath of allegiance. And your duty is not complete. When is anyone's duty complete, Mrs. Freeman?"

"All right, all right," Alice said, "but why do you need us any more? Why can't you take over?"

I lit a cigarette.

Mason Brown said, "Because you are the only contact we have with Oakes. If I went to Santa Serena, a small town of Danes, how could I hope to conceal myself? Our whole object, Mrs. Freeman, is to avoid arousing any suspicion in Oakes's mind, so that through him we can reach this other man."

"Friday," I said.

He looked at me and nodded. "Let us call him that," he said.

Alice said, "But why can't you trace him through the

108

boatmen? In fact, if you were already watching the boat why didn't you at the time?"

Mason Brown looked at her steadily for a moment and then suddenly he grinned at her like a school kid.

"You're the second person to ask me that this evening. The first was my boss. In fact, I'm in the doghouse over it. They slipped one over on me going to the beach like that. But by a great stroke of luck you people can help save the day."

I watched to see if Mason Brown's tactics were melting Alice any. I was beginning to develop quite a respect for his line. But Alice was not that easy.

She said, "It's still not too late. All those fishermen on the boat know him. Friday, I mean. Trace him through them."

Mason Brown gave a little sigh and got to his feet.

He said, "I only wish that were possible, Mrs. Freeman, but the Russian spy system is such that it isn't. However, I can see that I'm wasting my time so I'll say good-by."

He held out his hand to her.

She was on her feet as fast as he and shaking his hand.

"I'm sorry, too, Mr. Mason Brown. But I'm sure you'll manage without us."

I said, "Hold your horses. How do you mean about the Russian spy system?"

Alice sent me a look but I ignored it, looking steadily at Mason Brown.

He smiled a little, waved the thing aside.

"You never read Foote's *Story of a Russian Spy?* It's all in there. He was head of their ring in Switzerland through the war."

He chuckled, as though he was just having an aimless chat that meant nothing to him one way or the other. "He sent Moscow daily bulletins of all German troop movements and strategy, piped direct from German headquarters. Imagine it! And Stalin still couldn't win without us."

Alice said, "It sounds very interesting, Mr. Mason Brown. We must get the book."

Her tone was final and definite. I began to think it was time to show that I wore pants too.

I said, "Honey, if it's true what Mr. Mason Brown says, that Friday can't be traced through the fishermen, we've obviously got to help."

I turned to Mason Brown.

"Could you explain why that's so?"

"They operate through a system of cut-outs. Briefly, it means that no one knows his neighbor. In this case it's 90 per cent sure that the fishermen won't know anything of Friday and certainly won't have any knowledge of Oakes's existence. Oakes's orders would have been to watch for the boat and stay hidden from the crew among the bathers. So the only man who has to know Friday's whereabouts is Oakes. And there's another thing."

He sat down suddenly, then appeared to remember himself, and looked up at Alice who was still standing.

"If you'll excuse me?"

Alice sighed and looked at us both sitting down, and sat down too and said, "Go ahead."

"Well," said Mason Brown, "as you may know, in the field of espionage and counterespionage, a constant battle is going on between the two sides, the one trying to infiltrate new agents, the other trying to discover them. Both sides know that eventually most agents are discovered, so this process goes on all the time. We know a great number of their agents. But at the same time there are many who have been brought in recently that we do not know. This lead of yours constitutes probably the best we have at present to the newest ring. To land a man by submarine

110

suggests both his importance and also a certain sense of urgency. Is that clear?"

"Clear and impressive, Mr. Mason Brown. Don't you think so, dear?"

Alice said, "Just what shall we do?"

Mason Brown gave her a little smile of unspoken thanks, then turned to me.

"How soon could you get a vacation?"

"We'd been planning to include Thanksgiving, but I guess I could take it earlier."

"This coming week?"

"I'd have to ask French in the morning, see what he'd say. Everyone else has already taken theirs except the two skiers, and they —"

"Vacation, vacation," Alice cut in. "We were only asked to drop in at most. You can't drop in for a vacation."

"Honey, first let's find out what Mr. Mason Brown has in mind. Then —"

"It's quite simple," Mason Brown said.

I liked the way he took over, polite but firm.

"I want you to use your wits to establish contact as best you can, and to maintain it, without arousing suspicion, of course, and observe. If you should see anything, anything at all, that you think might be in the very slightest degree of help to me, then let me know. But on no account, and I repeat on no account, are you to take any kind of independent action except to communicate with me. Right?"

"Right. But of course I don't know what kind of reception we'll get."

"No," Alice said.

And that was all she said. I ignored it. Mason Brown, of course, had to ignore it. I wondered what he had pieced together about Liza.

And then he said, "Tell me, you never heard anything

111

further about either Oakes or his sister, or I should say his wife, from that day you left till today?"

Alice lit a cigarette.

I said, "Once, not long after we were married, my wife and I discussed it and we decided that I should write a letter to Dr. Linden. Just to make sure that things were all right with her. In view of my promise to her adopted father."

I wondered why I was telling Mason Brown all this, and realized that I valued his opinion of me, that I didn't want him to think that I was carrying any torch for Liza.

I remembered the day so well as I was speaking, Alice waking me up in the middle of the night, hitting me with a pillow and saying "Goddam it, if I have to marry a man with a conscience we might as well do it right." I blinked and asked her what the heck she was talking about, and she said that I had called Liza's name the last seven nights in a row, so I'd better write and find out if she was all right and get it out of my system. Which I did, both, though Alice, being female, maybe had some pinpricky reservations about the latter part.

"The letter came back from the doctor saying that she had just returned alone from abroad after an unsuccessful trip to find her family, but that she seemed well and happy and was busy with her horses and that there was no need for me to concern myself. And that's all I know."

"No mention of Oakes at all?"

"None."

Mason Brown thought a moment. Then he got to his feet.

"Well, that's it for now. Let me know in the morning when you can leave." He held out his hand. "Naturally, the sooner the better," he added.

I shook hands.

"If not this week we'll be able to make it by next week at the latest, I'm sure."

Alice said, "Don't give it a thought, Mr. Mason Brown. Our little family will dig up the whole network for you by Saturday week."

Mason Brown gave her one of his swift smiles and said, "You know, Mrs. Freeman, it wouldn't surprise me one bit if you did just that."

I saw him out to his car. As he put his finger on the starter he said casually, "I didn't like to say this in front of your wife, but of course you won't rely at all on Mrs. Oakes's discretion. What I mean is that a man's wife is just that."

I said, "I've been thinking about that. He must have fooled her completely. It beats me, that marriage, but I'll bet my last dollar she can't know of his activities."

He said, "I realize how you must feel. That's why I said what I did. In matters of security one has to be rigid, as you know, and regard everyone as a possible enemy until proved the opposite." He smiled amiably and said, "The reverse of our legal practice, isn't it?" and drove off with a wave of his hand.

When I got back in the house Alice was already undressed and brushing her hair at the mirror.

She said, "What else did Mr. Mason Brown have to impart?"

I took off my coat and hung it up and sat down to unlace my shoes.

"Just about watching everything, like the mail and so on."

She got up and switched off the little light on the dressing table and got into bed.

"Didn't he warn you against Liza at all?"

I took off my second shoe, put it beside the first, and went over to the bed and held her by the shoulders and looked in her eyes.

"Darn you, Alice, yes he did. Between the two of you, you'd think I was the original Don Juan or something."

She kissed me.

"Just something," she said.

She lay back in the bed. Her eyes were looking past me at the picture on the wall opposite. It was Liza's painting.

She said, "Now I suppose I'll get to see that goddam lake."

7

We left ten days later.

When we reached the San Marcos Pass and came down the wild hills to the floor of the valley we followed it along till we reached the lead to the Santa Serena. Approached from this direction it was some thirty miles less to Red Barns than by the coast route via Santa Serena itself.

I had thought at first that we should take the coast route and stay the night at the Santa Serena Inn before going to the ranch, but then we decided to take the bull by the horns and go first to the ranch itself.

Mason Brown had left complicated instructions for whenever I needed to call him. The first thing that we had to know was where we would be staying, whether or not Liza and Johnny could be brought to put us up at the ranch, if they had the room, or whether we should have to go on to the inn, in which case it would make it that much more difficult to return to the ranch and spy on Johnny.

The children were in a state of excitement. There had been some debate about leaving them behind because of any possible danger, but in view of what Mason Brown said about the fishermen not being connected with Johnny we could see none, and in any case Alice's folks had gone to Denver so we had nowhere to leave them, even if we had wished to.

Janie had only once been away before. That was two years back, when she was three and we had flown to Denver to see Grandmother Mounts, and Janie seemed to reason ever since then that there were only two places in the world, home, and Grandmother Mounts's place, which was reached by going through the sky. This had caused endless fights between her and Pete who was full of scorn at first, but had now reached a philosophical outlook about the mental capacity of his sister. Janie had matured from three to five, but there still existed relics of confusion on the subject.

"Why can't Gramunts fly here to meet us?" she wanted to know.

Alice and I left it to Pete, who was sitting in the back with her. It was more interesting that way, and much less tiring.

Pete said, "She's too old to fly."

I put a hand on Alice's knee to stop her exploding.

Janie said, "Stuff. Everybody flies to heaven when they die."

Pete was unruffled.

"There's no place for her to land around here," he said. "No airport."

"Why can't she land in the field by that cow?"

I slowed for the intersection and read the sign which said, Santa Serena ten miles straight on and Happy Valley to the right. I remembered the intersection at once, although I had not seen it for ten years and then from the other direction. I turned up right. It was only two miles to Red Barns.

"Where are you going now, Dad?" Pete asked.

"Remember the man who saved you in the water? He lives right by here. I thought I'd drop in and say hello."

"He didn't really save me. How far is it?"

116

"Not far. Look, you can see the trees from here, on that rise over there, see?"

Alice began to powder very carefully.

Janie said, "There's no house. Will Gramunts be in the trees?"

"The house is behind the trees. There are all kinds of buildings. It's a ranch."

"That's good," Pete said. "Will they have a rodeo for us?"

"I don't think it's that kind of ranch. Last time I was here they just had race horses and sheep."

Alice said, "Things change. Janie, take your finger out of your mouth and fasten your dress."

"Sheep," Pete said. "That's stinky. Eddie Whalen says no respectful man has sheep."

"Respectable, Pete. You see, Eddie's father is a cattle rancher from Arizona and they have strong ideas about that. But if there weren't any sheep ranches how would we eat leg of lamb ever?"

"What's that?" Janie asked.

Alice said, "You see, it's been a long time, Pop. Slow down, you'll overshoot the gate if that's it. Red Barns, it says."

"That's it and I won't. Relax, honey."

"What's everyone nervous for?" Pete asked.

I turned in the driveway over the cattle guard.

"Why do they have cattle bars without cattle?" Pete asked.

"Everyone has some cattle. They just don't have many, or didn't. Maybe they do now."

The driveway seemed unchanged, down over the little bridge with the tubs, then winding up the hill toward the paddock of brood mares. Only now I didn't see any brood mares. The notice at the circle entrance was still there, PLEASE DRIVE SLOW. I felt my heart pounding for no reason.

117

For a moment I thought of driving round the circle and straight out again.

I stopped in front of the house gate. There was nobody around.

"Race horses," Pete said. "Black yet."

There were three of them in the circle pasture. I wondered who they were, but I could not tell. They all looked like Black Mark to me.

Alice said, "Don't say 'black yet' like that. It doesn't mean anything."

She turned to me.

"Are you going to the door?"

"Yes."

I switched off the motor.

"Looks like they're out."

"Eddie Whalen always says yet," Pete said.

I said, "You can say, 'It looks as if they are not home yet.' That's the way to say yet, understand?"

I got out and started toward the garden gate.

Janie said, "But they are home yet. There's a stranger lady."

We turned and looked where Janie was pointing. There was a woman coming toward us, round the end of the big barn.

Alice turned to the children.

"Now listen to me, kids. No one asks for bubble gum. Or candy. Understand?"

It was Liza all right. You could tell by the walk and the hair. It had the same sheen, the hair. She was wearing jeans and an old brown shirt and carrying a bucket. I couldn't see her face properly until she came closer, nearer to the circle. And yet I suppose that I must have got an impression of it even in the distance, in the way that one does, because even before she came close up to us I could tell

118

that there had been a lot of change. You couldn't say what change exactly. Just change.

At first she didn't recognize me as I walked toward her. You could see that she was trying to figure out who we all were, strange man with family, probably someone come to book a stallion or what have you.

In the time before she recognized me, the noncommittal look of doubtful welcome was still there, and then she nearly dropped the bucket.

"Why, Sam!" she said. "Sam Freeman!"

She put the bucket down and looked at me and came up and held out both hands, and I knew that if Alice hadn't been there in the car she would have kissed me without thinking.

I took her hands. It was good to see her eyes laugh like that.

"Hullo, Liza!"

"What brought you up here, Sam?"

"It's my vacation, so we took Johnny at his word and dropped by on our way."

She looked puzzled.

"Johnny? Did you meet Johnny somewhere?"

"I guess he forgot to tell you. We bumped into him the other day and he said you were married and told us to drop by."

It was obvious that Johnny had not said a word to her about it, and I felt strangely pleased. If ever I had had any doubts about her being involved in anything wrong they were gone now.

I said, "Come and meet Alice."

She said, "That I would like very much."

I took her up to the car and introduced them to each other and watched them shake hands and smile at each other. Alice said, "I told Sam that we ought to phone first, but he insisted on driving right on. I hope we didn't come at an awkward time."

Liza laughed. It was a serene laugh. That was the change in her. She was serene. Suddenly I got the strangest feeling, a feeling that the whole thing about Johnny must have been a mistake. For Liza to exude that feeling, married to Johnny for a year, things must be all right.

Liza was saying to Alice, "All times are the same on a ranch. Probably no one would have heard the phone anyway. Are these your children?"

"Yes."

Alice introduced the kids. They were hopping to get out of the car, but they were polite.

Pete said, "How do you do, Mrs. Oakes. You have a very nice place."

Liza said, "Thank you. You haven't seen much of it yet."

Janie said, "Mrs. Oakes, is Gramunts asleep?"

Alice said, "Darling, Gramunts won't be here now. But we're going to have a lovely time just the same."

Pete said, "She thinks her grandmother is here some place. Can I speak to the black horses?"

I let them out of the car.

Liza said, "You can play with these horses all you want. They are not moody at all."

"What's moody?" Janie asked Pete, as they walked away together toward the horses.

"It's like old Mr. Kruger at the drugstore," Pete said.

Janie said, "He gave me some candy once."

The voices of the children got fainter.

It seemed strange, standing there with Alice and Liza together, it seemed very strange. The only two women in my life that had ever meant anything. And now they had met. I was feeling kind of glad just then that it had happened, this meeting, and yet I was aware of a fearful feeling

120

not so deep down below the surface, not so much a feeling to do with the girls or anything in particular, but a much more important feeling, to do with life itself, a feeling somehow connected with doom.

It came and went, and we were still standing there by the car in the sunlight, laughing and talking together and watching the children in the distance on the rail making up to the horses.

Liza said, "Come on in. They'll be all right. The men will look after them." She opened the wicket and we followed her into the front garden. "I can't think why Johnny didn't tell me he met you. Of course he's been very busy lately." She looked at me. "He's in partnership with Max now in the soup business. It's all doing wonderfully."

She was proud of him. Bygones were bygones with a vengeance, I thought, as I watched the carriage of her head as she walked along the path beside Alice. I wondered what Alice was thinking, but I couldn't tell. I never could with Alice.

She said, "This place is really lovely. What are those tall blue flowers called?"

It was the same time of year, and there they were, the same flowers, growing against the house on either side of the front door. At any moment now I almost felt as though I would see the old man standing in the doorway again.

"Those are lilies of the Nile," Liza said. "Agapanthus. I've had to learn that because everyone always asks." She laughed and opened the door and called out, "Johnny! Where are you, Johnny?"

Johnny's voice called out.

"Right here, baby, in the study. What's new?"

His voice sounded cheerful and relaxed.

"Sam Freeman and his family are here," Liza called. "Why didn't you tell me you met them?"

There was a little silence. Then the sound of a chair being pushed back, and his footsteps approaching. When he came in he was in control of himself, whatever might have been his initial reaction. He had a genial smile of welcome on his face, the perfect host, delighted to welcome us.

He advanced toward us with outstretched hand.

"Well, well," he said. "This is indeed a pleasant surprise. Nice to see you again, Mrs. Freeman."

He shook hands with Alice and she said, "We took you at your word, you see."

"Glad you did." He shook hands with me. "Sam, what do you know?"

I said, "It's my vacation. We're taking the children up the coast, fishing here and there as we go."

Liza said, "How wonderful! Why don't you stay here and fish the lake? There's plenty of trout, and the guest house is empty." She tucked her arm in Johnny's and gave it a little excited squeeze. "Wouldn't that be fine, Johnny?"

Johnny smiled at her and ruffled her hair and looked at us and said, "How about that?"

It was as easy as that. You couldn't tell if his endorsement had the same enthusiasm in it as her invitation or not. You just could not tell.

I said, "Well, that certainly is nice of you." I put what I hoped was the right amount of hesitation in my voice. "But we can't inflict a whole family on you at a minute's notice like this."

I looked at Alice and she picked it up.

She laughed and said, "Sam's a sucker for trout all right, but we only just dropped by to thank you again about Pete."

Johnny laughed, quick and hearty.

He said, "Of course you will stay. Happens all the time

122

— friends dropping in. We ranchers are like that, you know, aren't we, baby?"

Liza looked at him and her pride of him showed clearly. I did not think I would ever have lived to see such a day, and I found myself praying that we were wrong about him as I watched Liza just then, praying for her sake.

She said, "Then that's all fixed. What's this about Pete and why haven't I heard anything?"

I said, "Heroes don't talk. Johnny pulled him out of a bad wave at Santa Monica. Did a mighty fine job, too. That was how we met."

She looked prouder than ever.

"When was all this?"

"Sunday week."

She stared at Johnny.

"Sunday week! But that was when you went to the airport to meet Steve!"

He said, "That's what put it out of my head. It was so hot that I stopped off for a quick dip on the way down, and then meeting Steve's plane and everything I didn't give it another —"

"Johnny! You promised me!"

She was mad. She forgot us, she was that mad.

"You promised me!" she said again.

"Baby, I didn't get over ninety once. Truly." He turned to us. "She never realizes what time you can make in a Jag."

"Oh yes I do. I drive it plenty. And I know darn well you couldn't have made it to the airport with a swim, too, unless you were doing more. Why, you'd have to have flown."

She really cared if he broke his neck or not. She really cared.

He gave a little sigh.

"All right. Now I'll have to tell you. I was late for the plane."

She stared at him.

"But it was his welcome, Johnny!"

For a moment I caught in her eyes now a look of old, a look that I knew, but with a difference. Whereas in the old days there would have been a bitterness there because of her discovery of his irresponsibility, the bitterness of a girl at being let down, now it was the resigned expression of a woman who knows her man.

She said, "And I let you talk me out of coming."

"He didn't mind waiting. Truly he didn't." He gave her a quick little pat on the shoulder. "Look, I'll call him to meet our friends, shall I?"

He went to the door without waiting for an answer and called, "Steve!"

Liza turned to us.

"Forgive us for being so rude," she said.

I said, "Alice and I do it all the time."

The door across the dining room opened, the door of the room that used to be Liza's bedroom in the old days, and a man came out.

"You want me, Johnny?" he asked.

He came toward us across the dining room. From where I was standing behind Liza I was in line so that I could see him all the way across the dining room over her shoulder, and I think I recognized him almost as soon as I saw him, although I had not been able to describe him very well when questioned by Mason Brown. But as he came closer and stood in the doorway, I knew for sure that it was Friday, the swimmer from the boat.

There was no mistaking him, seeing him again, and I saw the reason that he had been difficult to describe, because of the very indefiniteness of his face structure. It was not

124

that it was weak, but simply that none of the features was pronounced. He was of medium build as we had said, between thirty-five and forty, and Alice had been right about his hair — it was dark brown, not quite black.

I knew, of course, that he could not recognize me because he had not set eyes on me, but I waited very carefully for his eyes to rest on Alice. I watched them for the slightest sign of recognition that would show he remembered her in the sea during the moment of his arrival. I realized that Johnny had no idea that he had met Alice in the sea, or that I had seen him there, or he would not have so boldly asked him in. But I knew that if Friday, or Steve, recognized her, it would give us away.

I could not warn Alice, and I could not watch her either to see if she would recognize him and give herself away, because I had to watch his eyes. And, as they passed inquiringly over us all, I saw that there was no slightest sign of recognition in them when he saw her there, and it passed through my mind that she had been wearing her swimming cap then, whereas now her hair was loose and down around her head so that it would frame it and make quite a difference, especially to someone who had only seen her as briefly as he had.

"I didn't hear anyone come in," he said, as he stood in the doorway.

His voice was quiet and unassuming, and, as Alice had told Mason Brown, it had a trace of a foreign quality in it if you listened carefully, just a trace.

Liza said, "Steve — I want you to meet some friends, Alice and Sam Freeman."

And then she turned to us and said, "This is my brother, Steve Donniken."

8

I remembered the old man's will. "To Liza Oakes, nee Donniken."

I remembered Dr. Linden's letter, saying that Liza had just returned from an unsuccessful search for her family.

I remembered the photograph in Liza's bedroom, the one that I had studied while she was lying unconscious there in the bed after the accident. Liza, the little girl of four, the two parents, and the brother, the figure squatting down, his face turned away from the camera, beckoning to a cocker spaniel.

He was about sixteen then. That would make the age right. And the hair. The brother's hair in the picture had been dark too, although you could not tell if it were dark brown or black.

And I thought that Johnny had planned things well. He had planned things very well, he and the late Joe Stalin between them. And I wondered how he had sold the deal to Liza, so that he had first got her to marry him, and then got her to believe that her brother had been found.

Perhaps he had only had to do the first part of it. And then the rest would be easy, once she was his . . .

I must have shown a reaction in my face because I caught them all looking at me.

126

Friday, or Steve, was holding out his hand. He too was looking at me, puzzled a little.

I took his hand because I had to.

I said, "I had no idea. I had no idea."

Liza said, "You mean Johnny didn't tell you?"

Johnny said, "I didn't have time. You know that."

Liza said, "Steve! You never told me that Johnny kept you waiting at the airport."

He looked at her gravely. I knew that he did not know what she was talking about, but he covered it by a look of solemnity.

"No," he said, "no, I didn't tell you."

Johnny said, "I made him promise, Liza." He turned to Steve. "The cat's out of the bag, Stevie, boy. I met these people on the beach just before I met you and invited them up here. That's how she found out that I stopped off for a swim and was late meeting your plane."

Steve gave a bland smile. I don't know if the word is bland or urbane. You can pay your money and pick your choice, for it was one of those smiles a banker gives a frosty client.

He said, "You see, all is discovered." He turned to Liza, "We men have to stick together you know, dear."

She said, "You certainly do that." She turned to us.

"Steve is helping Johnny with his soup business. I hardly ever see him. You'd think he was Johnny's brother, not mine."

Alice laughed politely.

"I'd better go see after the kids," she said.

"Let's do," Johnny said. "How's my boy?"

"Fine," Alice said. "Just fine."

Steve said, "You have children?"

"Two," I said. "A boy and a girl."

"That's just how it should be, isn't it?" Steve said.

Liza said, "Tell you what. Why don't you drive over to the guest cottage and unpack, then the kids can have their dinner and then we can have ours when they're all through."

Alice looked at me now.

"Maybe we should call George and find out for sure if he's meeting us or not?" She turned to Liza. "A friend of ours is supposed to be fishing with us for a couple of days and we promised to call him and make sure he doesn't get off a day early."

"To tell him where we located," I said.

Liza said, "You want to use the phone?"

"Not right now," I said. "It's too early for George right now. Later if we may." I looked at Alice. "I'll move the car over while you get the kids' dinner."

"All right," she said.

There wasn't anything else she could say right then. I knew that she had recognized Friday. And she wanted to get out as fast as she could. But I knew we should not do that before contacting Mason Brown. And he might want us to stay and introduce him. Maybe as a fishing friend at that.

We were all outside now, watching the kids with the horses over by the paddock. There were a couple of men with them in Western hats and jeans.

"Are those the same men you always had?" I asked Liza. She laughed.

"One's a son and the other's a grand nephew, if there is such a thing. You didn't see the others I imagine?"

"No. How time flies."

She was walking along beside me now and Alice was between Johnny and Steve. They were a few yards away so I lowered my voice and said to Liza, "When did you hear about Steve? How did it all happen? I didn't like to ask in front of him."

"I'm glad you didn't," she said. "He doesn't care to talk much about it. Oh, Sam, it must have been horrible. Just horrible."

"Your father and mother?" I asked. I felt bad asking that, but I wanted to learn what I could fast.

"Oh, they were lucky," she said in a quiet voice. "They were drowned almost at once. The little boat turned over you know. And he was washed ashore and picked up by the Abyssinians. And then sold to the Arabs, just like Dad said. Just like he always said."

I thought, God damn you, Johnny Reschetnikoff, God damn you.

"And then," I said, "I suppose the Russians got him in the Caucasus some place and held him till he escaped?"

She looked at me.

"How did you know?"

"I just figured it must have been that way," I said. "And he caught the accent a little."

She nodded.

"He does seem a little strange, but what else could one expect after such a life?"

I said, "You know, Liza, doesn't it seem a bit incredible for such a thing to happen in this century — shipwrecked survivors being sold as slaves to Arab dhows, slave caravans up to the Caucasus and all that? I remember the old man saying how it used to happen when he was young, in the last century, but surely it didn't still go on in our lifetime?"

She looked at me.

"It went on right up to the Italian war with Abyssinia, and maybe still does. When I went to Massaua I found out plenty."

"But you didn't trace Steve then?"

"I got onto a man in the bazaar in Massaua who led me to another in Djibouti. There I lost the trail, but it was enough to convince me there was still a chance of their being alive. But I couldn't get further."

"And then Johnny helped you after you got married?"

"Johnny? Oh no, he couldn't do anything. The first I knew was a letter from Steve saying he had escaped from Russia and was safely back in New York. But Johnny has been so wonderful about him coming here. You know how it is in a marriage — you don't like to clutter it with relations, especially such a stranger, almost. But Johnny has been wonderful and helpful, trying to draw Steve out of himself. In every way, Johnny has been wonderful."

The men were taking the horses in from the paddock and the kids were running toward us. I was glad there was no time for comment. We waited for the others to come up as the kids ran to us.

Pete said, "Dad, they're not all race horses. Mr. West says they've got plenty of saddle horses we can ride!"

Janie said, "I gave them some carrots. Horses eat carrots without putting them in the press."

Pete said, "She means a pressure cooker. She means they eat them raw. Dad, can't we go riding? We can both ride well enough now to go riding. Mrs. Stokes said so in Santa Monica."

Alice said, "You know, Sam, I really do think we ought to get on to San Luis Obispo in case George should turn up there."

I knew she wanted me to say we had to leave. But I did not want to until I had talked to Mason Brown.

I said, "Well, I don't see how he can be there before tomorrow evening."

Liza said, "But you must stay at least one night anyway.

130

Then we can all ride up to the lake and Johnny can take the kids in his speedboat, can't you, Johnny?"

"Sure," Johnny said. "Only it will disturb the fish."

Liza said, "They can fish first in the rowboat and then go in the speedboat. How's that?"

"Just so long as I can get to Max's by lunchtime," Johnny said. "I've an appointment then."

Alice said, "I'm sure it's putting you out too much. We really have to be in San Luis Obispo by evening."

Liza said, "Then I have a solution. We'll all ride up early so that you can get in the fishing and the speedboat, and then we'll all go down to lunch at the inn from there, and after lunch you can leave from the inn. It's right on the coast highway so you can easily make it to San Luis Obispo by evening."

Pete said, "Please let's stay, Dad, and you can fish in the lake."

Janie said, "I want to stay. I want to sleep with the horses. They're more fun than fishes."

I said to Liza, "I think it will be fine, if you're sure it's not putting you out too much then."

Alice sent me a look.

Liza said, "Then it's all settled."

The kids were jumping up and down.

Alice said sharply, "Say how do you do to Mr. Oakes, children. And this is Mr. Donniken."

Pete looked at Johnny.

"Have you really got a speedboat?"

Janie said, "You're the man who saved Pete from a drowning, I think."

Pete turned to her.

"I wasn't drowning, stupid girl."

I said, "Say how do you do to Mr. Donniken."

"How do you do," Pete said.

Janie looked at him and said nothing. Friday squatted down and chucked her under the chin.

"What's your name, little girl?" he asked.

Janie still didn't answer. Then suddenly she burst into tears and ran to Alice.

"I don't like him," she said.

There was a little silence.

Alice said, "I'm afraid they're getting tired and hungry. You know how it is."

Friday was standing up again. I got a strange feeling. Everyone was talking at once now, and as I watched Friday I saw him looking at Janie out of the corner of his eye, studying her with a thoughtful expression. It was just for a second, and then he was laughing at something Liza was saying and we were all walking back toward the house and I thought it was just that the man's feelings had been hurt. And I thought it surprising that he had any.

Liza was saying to Alice, "I'll have their dinner ready right away. By the time you're unpacked it will be ready for them."

Alice said, "Fine. We'll go and tidy up and I'll bring them right over."

"Johnny can show you, won't you, Johnny?"

"You bet," Johnny said.

Steve and Liza went back into the house. I drove the car over to the guest cottage while Johnny took Alice and the children along the path. The place looked just the same. There were scarcely any changes that I could remember. All her pictures were there still. It seemed incredible after so long, almost as if time had stood still.

Johnny left us after he had shown us around and said, "If you need anything just give a yell and someone will come over. Better still, give this a shake." He shook the cowbell fixed against the wall by the door. It gave forth

132

a sound such as I had not heard since I was at a farmhouse in Sicily during the war.

Johnny liked the jingle of it. He did it again just for the heck of it and stood listening to it for a moment with his head cocked on one side and a strange expression in his eyes.

He said, "I found that on a ranch in Santa Maria. The man said it was used by the Spaniards who lived there before the conquest."

"What conquest was that?" I asked him.

He looked at me a moment and smiled in that way that he had always had, the way that he had smiled when I first met him, that day at the inn, more with his lips than with his eyes, and he said, "The American conquest, what else?"

Then he laughed and turned on his heel and walked away back to the ranch. He walked so easily, in the characteristic effortless way that he had, as though he had not a care in the world or an unworthy thought in his head, a man with a ranch, peacefully living in Southern California and going about his business like any other self-respecting citizen.

Alice was standing in the doorway watching him too.

"Just like a cat," she said softly.

Inside we could hear the children running about and exclaiming to each other, and for a moment we were alone together, the first time since we had arrived.

She put her head against my shoulder, as we stood together in the doorway looking across the fields toward the hills on the horizon, and she said, "Oh, Sam, it doesn't seem possible, to have such horror in a place like this. Darling, we ought not to have stayed. We should have gone when we saw him. We should have gone."

She was trembling a little against me. I put my arm

133

around her shoulders. The evening air was cooler now and the daylight was going from the sky.

I said, "Don't worry, baby, nothing's going to happen. He didn't recognize you. We can't leave till I've got in touch with Mason Brown. I'll call him soon as I can and see what he says. He may need us here to introduce him as a friend. Come on now, let's get busy."

But she was still trembling.

She said, "You must call him right away. You must. You tell him we're not staying after tomorrow whatever he says. I don't think that creature recognized me, but he might any minute."

"All right. I'll tell him. I'll go down to the village. It's too risky from here. You tell Liza I went for some medicine for Janie. Say I'll be right back."

"Sam."

"Yes?"

"You wouldn't risk our staying here if it wasn't for her. You want to protect her."

There was a small effort of pulsation in my chest, as if from running. I said, "I'm sorry you said that."

"Isn't it true?"

I took my arms away.

"You think so. I don't. Perhaps we're both too prejudiced to tell. I'll ask Mason Brown. Be seeing you."

I walked down the steps and got in the car without looking at her. I thought, that was a hell of a thing for her to say. I started the motor. And then I thought that I was reacting too much if it did not have some truth in it. I looked back toward the doorway. But she had gone back in the house. I could hear her calling the children. I let in the clutch and drove toward the ranch house. As I was passing the front gate on my way round the driveway

Johnny was standing in the middle of the drive, so I had to stop.

"Where d' you think you're going?" he asked. He had a grin on his face.

I said, "Janie has to have a prescription made up. It won't take me long."

"Okay, we'll go together. I have to go see Max before dinner anyway. Let's take my car. It will be a lot quicker."

I could not think of anything to say to that without arousing suspicion. I got out of the car and walked with him toward the shed. I wondered what his thoughts were, but there was nothing you could tell. He was saying, "I keep her by the shed mostly instead of by the garage because I'm always fiddling around. That's a motor for you, that Jag. You know them?"

"A client of mine has one. I've ridden in it."

It was standing under the overhung roof outside the shed, where the tractor had stood in the old days. It was clean and black and shining. He had cleaned up the shed too. Now there was a fourth wall built with a padlocked door so you could not see inside the shed any more and it all looked fresh and neat from the outside with new paint.

I said, "You've changed things a bit I see."

He climbed into the sports car and pressed the starter and the motor opened up. He said, "Lots of things have changed now. Hop in."

I got in beside him. He let in the clutch and made a skid turn round the shed.

"Don't kill me just yet," I said.

He grinned.

"We'll postpone it, huh?"

Liza came running out as he reached the front gate of the house. She waved at him to pull up.

"Where are you going, Johnny?"

"Sam has to get some medicine so I thought I'd speak to Max a minute."

"Well, don't be long and spoil the dinner."

He grinned at her.

"How soon you want us back? You name it."

"Johnny!" She looked at me and she was serious. "Sam, he's promised not over seventy."

"I'll watch it," I said.

She smiled at me and said to Johnny, "Oh, and if you're going to the drugstore, get me a jar of face cream, dear, will you?"

"You bet," Johnny said. "Anything else? No marketing, no mail, no clothes for the cleaners?"

She made a face at him.

"Listen, what I do want is some soup for the kids right now. I'm clean out. You've a sample case in the car, haven't you?"

He laughed and got out and went to open the turtle back. "You want a whole case?"

"One can, stupid. Or two, maybe."

He looked in the rumble and said, "I forgot, I emptied everything in cleaning the car. Tell Steve to get you a can from in there. He has a key." He climbed back in the car. "We're in a hurry, remember?"

"You remember, too," she laughed.

He blew her a kiss and drove off. She waved back at us, standing there watching us till we went through the gateway and turned down the hill out of sight.

They were for all the world like a perfectly normal happily married couple. Except maybe a little more in love, you might think.

Johnny drove down the hill and over the little bridge.

He said, "She's a henpecker all right, isn't she?"

136

"Well, seventy's not slow."

"It's nothing in this. Half what it can do."

He drove out the gate onto the highway and turned and put his foot down. The back of the seat hit me in the neck.

"I can make a right angle at darn near that. Watch this."

There was a right angle turn half a mile down the road. It was only a two-lane road. Across the field of alfalfa I could see the road quite clearly through a plain wire fence. There was nothing coming. Johnny swung out on his left lane, right to the edge of it as he approached the corner. He kept to his word and the needle stayed on the seventy mark. But it stayed there almost right into the corner. Then he double clutched down to third and braked to sixty and turned to cut across at a forty-five degree angle. As the car started on the new line he put his foot down on the gas again and passed the corner post at sixty-seven. Then he was headed straight for the left ditch. But he never let up his foot as he flicked the wheel over a little to the right. I felt the rear sliding toward the ditch. Then he countered the wheel a little and the slide ceased and we were headed straight along the road, picking up to seventy again now as he changed back to high.

He turned to me and smiled like a school kid with his first hot rod. "See what I mean?" he asked me.

"Must be some kind of a record, I'd say."

He shook his head.

"Now I'll tell you something real funny. Liza can beat it herself, when she's in that mood."

"I certainly wouldn't have suspected it of her," I said. "But then of course I don't know her as you do."

He drove on in silence for a while. Lights were on now in the scattered houses that we passed. The outline of the little rolling hills against the sky was not so sharp as it had been earlier.

137

Johnny switched on his headlights.

He said, "I know why you came up."

I was lying as low down in my seat as I could because of the cold wind. His remark made me wish to sit upright. But I didn't sit upright. I stayed as I was and said, "You do?"

"Sure. That fishing story didn't fool me one bit. It was what I said on the beach about Liza and me being married. It threw you at the time. I saw it." He looked across at me, then back at the highway. "You wanted to make sure that Liza was happy with me, didn't you?"

The needle was resting steadily at seventy, glowing red now that he had turned on the lights. I watched the figures of the mile tenths moving up and figured out that there had to be one every five and a piece seconds.

I said, "Didn't know my face was that expressive."

He laughed. He was actually pleased with himself.

"It's not only that. You hate my guts. So you wouldn't have come except that you felt guilty at having turned Liza down that night."

"She tell you that?"

He nodded, lifting his foot slightly from the accelerator. The road was twisting around the low hills. There was a glimpse of the Santa Serena lights ahead.

"She said that you were already in love with Alice. I made her tell me after we were married. You see, I'd always wondered about that night. Remember when we left the dinner table and went in the kitchen?"

He spoke as if it were the memory of a friendly party. I wanted to hit him. I looked across the ploughed fields at the barns and the windmill by a stream curving in the hollow of the land. I couldn't see the water because it was too dark, but I knew that it was a stream by the contours and the brush growing.

138

I said, "Yes, I remember."

"I told her then that she'd best make a quick play for you if she wouldn't marry me. I think that she would have gone for you anyway."

The houses were clustering now, the respectable Danish American houses of the citizens of Santa Serena, spick and span and neat and innocent of traitors.

I said, "Where does all this lead to?"

He slowed for the village, made a left turn, and chuckled.

"To the drugstore," he said.

There were two or three cars parked diagonally near the corner, but Johnny found a space right outside the door of the drugstore. I climbed over the door on my side.

"If you want to go on and see Max and come back for me while I get the prescription made up it may save some time."

"That's okay," he said. He jumped out and joined me. "I can wait."

We walked in the store together. There was a man in a white coat behind the drug counter and a girl serving a woman at the cosmetics counter. There was a telephone booth in the far corner, back of the prescription counter.

I walked up the store to the man, and Johnny walked right along with me, whistling softly between his teeth, under his breath. It sounded like "When the Red Red Robin Goes Bob Bob Bobbin Along." He waved cheerfully at the girl behind the counter and said something in Danish to the woman who answered him stolidly. She was a stolid woman so you couldn't tell if she liked him or not. The girl smiled respectfully as she was making change for the woman. That was all there was to it as far as she was concerned.

Johnny said to the druggist, "Good evening, Eric, I want

you to meet a friend of mine, Mr. Freeman. He wants a prescription made up. Sam, this is Mr. Knudsen."

I said, "Hullo, Mr. Knudsen," and shook hands and summed him up.

He said, "It's a pleasure, Mr. Freeman."

He was a man in his late fifties, with the clear blue Danish eyes and a wide thoughtful forehead, and I liked him instantly. There was a certain reserve in his manner, but I had a hunch that this was to do with Johnny rather than with me and I decided to gamble on it.

I started to hunt through my pockets and said, "First, I've got to find the darn prescription."

The woman was going out and the girl was alone at the counter. I said to Johnny, "Didn't you have to get some face cream for Liza or something?"

"So I did."

He turned and went over to the girl. I whipped a pencil out and started writing on the paper I had all ready, words I had thought of during the drive just in case I could not phone.

I looked over at Johnny. He was talking to the girl.

I wrote:

GEORGE MASON BROWN. 3437 WILSHIRE APARTMENT B, LOS ANGELES. FRIDAY HERE AT RANCH STOP WE LEAVE TO- MORROW STOP COME AT ONCE. FREEMAN.

Knudsen was looking at me expectantly, awaiting the prescription. Johnny was still talking to the girl. I handed the paper and a five dollar bill to Knudsen.

I said, "Will you phone this telegram for me directly we've gone, please?"

He looked puzzled, took the paper and the bill and looked at it. Johnny had turned now, a package in his hands. I could see him in the little mirror hanging over the prescription counter. Knudsen was going to say something.

I picked up a bottle off the counter. It said Collyrium Eye Drops.

I said, "Thank you very much, Mr. Knudsen. I'm very much obliged to you. I'll take this just as it is. There's no need to wrap it up."

I couldn't tell if he saw that I was anxious about Johnny or not. But anyway he didn't say anything. Either he got it or it was all too fast for him. I didn't wait to find out. I turned away, holding the bottle in my hand with my finger over the label, and walked down the store to meet Johnny.

"All set," I said. "You too?"

He looked surprised.

"That was quick to make up a prescription."

"It wasn't on prescription after all. You can get it without. I never understand this thing about prescriptions anyway. Some places they'll give you things, some they won't."

"It probably depends on the percentage of drug in it," he said. "Some druggists are more literal than others."

He was quite unsuspicious, walking out of the store with me. He turned and waved to Knudsen.

"See you, Eric," he called.

I looked back. Knudsen was reading what I had written as it lay on the counter. He looked up and nodded, then went on reading. Johnny turned away and we walked over to the car. My hands were sweating. I put the bottle in my pocket and climbed in the Jaguar. Johnny got in his side and started the motor.

He said, "That girl is pretty dumb." Then he laughed. "Maybe it's just I'm an old married man these days."

"Good for you," I said. "Where to now?"

"Drop in on Max a moment. You remember him, that's where we first met, at the inn, remember?"

"That's right, I remember," I said.

He drove up the street and turned opposite Andresen's service station where I had rented the old Chevvy, and went down the three blocks to the inn. It all looked exactly the same as it did, as much as I could tell by the street lighting. Maybe there were more automobiles around and it was a little more built up, but there was no startling change. Santa Serena was still Santa Serena.

There were a lot of cars in the inn parking lot. Johnny pulled up beside a bus marked Special and we got out.

"Tourists," Johnny said. "They make round trips and stop here for meals. Max does well by them. I'm having a fight with him about them over my campaign. Come on in and see the fireworks."

I didn't know what he was talking about, but I went along with him just the same. I still had not seen anything to make me suspicious of anything he did. He was just living the life he had made for himself. Or rather himself and Friday. He had formed a wonderful background for Friday. The Danes might not like Johnny but they would all accept Liza's brother.

I thought that I was probably wasting time anyway. Now that we had found and reported Friday our job was done. Provided Knudsen sent the wire. And, I thought, even if he didn't, I would soon be able to reach Mason Brown by phone, even after we had left, for that matter. I kept remembering Alice's face and thinking that nothing was worth staying on up there any longer. We would go in the morning after we got back from the lake.

We went into the inn. The place was jammed, quite unlike the last time I had seen it, during the war, all that time ago. They had added on to it too. There was another big room running off the hall to the right, a second dining room, divided only by a low wall with pillared arches. People were everywhere, in the lobby, in the bar as we went through, looking at the curios, and filling both dining rooms.

I said, "Max must be coining it."

He nodded.

"We're doing well," he said. "But you should see how my department is growing. Of course you can only see that on paper. But I can tell you this. That since I've been with him, our soup sales have jumped 15 per cent."

"Sounds good enough."

I saw Max detach himself from a group by one of the curio tables and come up to us. I remembered his face at once. The years had not taken too great a toll. He was fatter but not too much so, and his eyes still held the same look of quick appraisal that I remembered at once now. But as he looked at Johnny I saw he was worried.

He said at once to Johnny, "I told you No over the phone, Johnny."

Johnny laughed.

"That's why I came down. If you won't, I will."

Max frowned.

"Look, there are forty-four of them in a busload." He waved his hand at the long table in the second dining room where they were all eating together. "Work it out, against the dinner profit, forty-four cans, why it's —"

Johnny cut in. "That's the point, Max, you mix two departments. The dinner profit is separate from the soup sales, can't you see?" He turned to me, put his hand on my arm and said to Max, "You probably don't remember, Max, but you introduced us in the first place, a long time ago — Sam Freeman."

He looked at me again now and a sudden flash came into his eyes.

"Indeed, but I do now," he said as we shook hands. "Even then he was trying to give away my soup, do you remember, Mr. Freeman?"

I laughed.

"Is he trying to do it again?"

"He won't stop. It gets worse and worse. Now he's started a hare-brained scheme to give a can to every tourist who comes here for the next month or so."

"No, Max, I'll settle for just one week and then wait and see if we get results. If we don't in seven busloads then we'll quit. How's that?"

"How can you prove results anyway? Those people probably come from all over the United States. They take a can of soup home. Maybe they give it away. Maybe they eat it. Maybe they like it. Are they going to tell their market to stock it?"

"Why not? An enthusiastic customer is the best salesman there is."

Max threw up his hands.

"You see?" he asked me. "You are in business, perhaps, yourself, Mr. Freeman?"

"Insurance business."

"Any business is business. I wish you could take Johnny here into your office, just for a month even, to pick up some rudiments of what's business and what isn't."

Johnny got riled up. He really got riled up at that one. You could almost see the hackles.

He said, "All right, Max. I'll pay for it myself. Cash." He put his hand in his pocket, then said, "No, take it out of my account. Forty-four cans. And tomorrow for the lunchtime bus I'll bring one of my own sample cases down.

And for all the rest I'll use my own samples too. It won't cost you a nickel."

He walked off across the room toward where the cases of soup were stacked against the wall in the same place as they had been before, leaving Max and me looking at each other.

Max said, "You are friends, you two?"

I said, "His wife is a friend of my wife's and mine. We are staying the night up there."

His face brightened.

"How is she?"

"Fine."

He nodded.

"She was looking radiant the other day. She came in to introduce her brother. Isn't it wonderful for her?"

"Wonderful. He isn't a bit like her, is he?"

"Well, of course, he is very reserved. But then that's not surprising, when you consider all the poor man went through."

"Tell me, doesn't it seem a little strange to you?"

"Strange?"

"I mean all that story of the slave caravans and everything?"

He looked at me, thoughtfully.

"To a stranger, it may be strange. Not to us in Santa Serena. You say you are her friend?"

"Indeed I am."

"But you did not meet the old man perhaps, Andrew?"

"I met him briefly. He was wonderful."

His face softened again.

"He was indeed wonderful. In Santa Serena, Mr. Freeman, you cannot walk a street, nor pass a single house, where dwells no love for Liza and Andrew. It was he who told us this story. It was his belief. It was why he adopted her. If there were any who doubted him then, there are none today. It is like a miracle."

"I see."

I was thinking, you son-of-a-bitch, Johnny Oakes. The miracle of Santa Serena. What better background for a spy.

I said, "And what about Johnny? Is he not included in the love of Santa Serena?"

Max's eyes followed mine. We watched him through the arches in the other room. He was going down the long table, giving each person a can of soup and a souvenir from the curio room, talking and laughing with each one in turn, the picture of the genial host and Santa Claus.

Max sighed a little. "I wish I could understand him. He loves to play with my soup. He loves to play with her ranch. At least he no longer plays with the girls since he returned. I suspect she made that a condition." He turned to me. "Why did he marry her, Mr. Freeman? Why did he come back here at all?"

I shrugged.

"Why did you give him a job?"

"She begged me. His self-respect, she said. That he had returned a new man." He sighed again. "Well, we shall see. How do you say it? If the leopard has changed his spots. I hope so, for her sake. We all do, for her sake."

"She never showed signs of falling in love those years he was gone?"

He shook his head, sadly.

"She worked, and loved us all, and worked. Encased herself in a glass of smiles. Then he returned. She did not send him away, as we all foretold. Then one day the glass was gone and she came alive again and married him. For this, Santa Serena is prepared to suffer him."

146

Johnny was coming toward us now from the other room. He was looking smug. I wanted to cut his throat.

He said, "There you are, Max, you see, they liked the soup so much they were grateful for the gift. And they promised to tell their markets back home. Could you sell it any cheaper way with salesmen?"

Max said, "We'll see what happens. Did you enter it up?"

"You bet. And starting tomorrow I'll use my own. Come on, Sam."

I nodded at Max who gave me a smile and a little shrug. Johnny was already striding through the lobby. I followed him out to the car. We both got in and he drove off. Nobody said a word. After a couple of blocks he said, "That Max. Stubborn like a Dane."

"That a Danish characteristic?"

"The whole bunch of them." He waved his hand at the houses. "Lot of mules, that's what they are."

"Maybe they think we are too."

"You mean Max said something against me, of course."

I said, "He was wondering why you came back to Santa Serena."

He turned his head toward me.

"And so are you."

I could not see his eyes in the dark, but I could see the outline of his head against the night sky. He turned his head back to the road again. It was a beautiful profile. It should have been on a coin.

"I will tell you, Sam. That night was the lowest ebb of my life. My father's death brought it home to me, how low I had sunk. I went away. I went East, I went to Europe, I went all over. I tried many kinds of work. All the time I knew I was just trying to escape from myself. I knew I had to come back to Santa Serena and face the music and Liza, square myself. The night I decided that I was a changed person. And I've stayed changed ever since. And I'll prove it to them yet. That's why I'm so steamed up about this selling idea. I'm going to prove to Max I'm good. And all the rest of them."

I was still watching the shape of his head. It was a beautiful profile. Yes, it should have been on a coin. It should have been on a ruble.

I said, "You'll convince them all right, if that's what you're set on."

"And you?" he asked.

"It's okay by me, now I know that everything's all right with Liza and you. It's nice for her, her brother turning up like that, isn't it? Amazing thing, after all these years."

"Isn't it? She told you the story, I expect?"

"Yes. Except how he escaped."

"Tell you the truth, I don't know too much of that myself. He hates to talk about it. Reticent kind of chap." He eased his foot on the accelerator pedal. "It's ironical, Liza thinking that I like him so much, when all the time I'm just going out of my way to be nice. The truth is he's getting to be in our hair a bit. I suppose you wouldn't have a job for him, would you, or know anyone?"

Oh, Johnny, oh, Johnny, oh.

"What does he do?"

"Christ, he just sits around in his room all the time. But I guess he's pretty smart."

"What makes you think so?"

"He survived, he escaped, and he's Liza's brother."

"Well, I don't know of anything, but why not try a little publicity? With a story like that, it might help."

His foot came up a fraction higher. The needle was down to forty now. We had only another mile or so to go.

Johnny said, "I don't think that would be at all fair to

148

him, Sam. He'd just hate it. You don't know him like I do.
I beg of you, don't let it get to the papers."

"Cross my heart, as far as I'm concerned. But the whole
village knows about it, don't they?"

He turned the right angle bend and zipped up the re-
maining piece of road to the ranch gates. I could almost
feel him smile.

He said, "They won't talk. He belongs to them, and
they're Danes."

He turned in at the gate.

I said, "So they do have some good characteristics?"

He laughed.

"I guess they do at that."

He swirled around the driveway and parked by the garden gate and jumped out.

"Come on," he called, like a kid, "I'm hungry and I'll
bet they've started."

I followed him up the garden to the house. There was a
smell of dinner.

There was the sound of laughter, Liza's laughter it was.
And the squealing of the children.

149

9

They were all in the dining room. Liza and Alice were still sitting at the table. Friday was crawling on all fours around the dining table. Janie was sitting astride his back, holding him by the ears. And Pete, dear Pete, was hitting him on the backside with a fly swatter, crying, "Trot, trot! Now you must trot!"

Janie squealed.

"Trot! Now you must trot!"

Friday began an undulating motion, bouncing Janie a little on his back. She fell off. He caught her and fell himself, tripping up Pete. They all fell in a heap together. Friday's face was solemn. He could have been enjoying himself. He said to Pete, "Now you be the horse."

Alice said, "Okay, kids, that's all. Time for bed."

Liza was still laughing. I caught a swift look at Johnny's face as we came in. He was definitely startled at Friday's behavior. But he quickly masked it.

He said, "How do you like being a horse, Stevie boy?"

Liza said, "He's been wonderful. Just wonderful."

Everyone started talking at once. The children ran up to me.

Janie said, "This man is coming riding too. He's coming riding to the lake with us."

Pete said, "I'm going to ride a brown horse and Janie's going to ride a paint horse."

150

Alice said, "Don't say 'this man,' Janie. Say 'Mister Donniken.'"

"Mister Donniken makes a good horse," Janie said.

Friday said, "We're going to stay friends, remember, Janie?"

She looked at him and put her finger in her mouth. She nodded and smiled suddenly and jumped up and down.

She said, "I'll call you Uncle Painthorse." She laughed and pointed her finger at him. "Uncle Paint!"

Alice took her by the hand.

"Come on now, that's all." She turned to Liza. "If I don't get them in now, they'll be awake all night. If you won't think me rude I'll stay with them and turn in, too. I've a bit of a headache."

"Of course," Liza said. "Have you everything you want?"

"Yes thanks," Alice said. "See you later, Sam. Thank you so much, Mr. Donniken. Good night, Mr. Oakes."

They said good night. She went to the door with the kids.

She said to me, "Did you get Janie's medicine?"

I followed her to the door and opened it. When we got outside, the kids ran on ahead. She said quickly, "Did you call him?"

I shook my head.

"Johnny was around. I slipped a wire to the druggist."

She looked alarmed.

"Can you trust him? Will he send it?"

I said, "I think so. Talk to you later." I said, louder, so they could hear through the open doorway, "I'll eat and come over as soon as I can."

She picked it up.

"Take your time," she laughed. "No hurry."

I closed the door.

Liza was saying, "Steve, you were wonderful! You should have seen him, Johnny."

"I did," Johnny said.

"What you saw was nothing," Friday said. "Tomorrow I shall have many bruises, I believe."

Liza was looking at him with a new admiration in her eyes.

"I believe so too," she said softly.

Johnny said, "Those kids really got you, didn't they, Steve? You really coming riding with us tomorrow?"

Friday said, "You never told me about the lake. I wish to see it. I thought maybe it would make an ideal place for us. To build a small guest ranch up there."

I caught a quick look between them.

Liza said, "Guest ranch. You can't fool me, Steve. You just want to be with those children."

Friday smiled, contriving a sheepish look. He turned to me.

"They are most charming, those children."

"Thank you," I said.

I wondered what he wanted with the lake, what type guests he would have up there. I could imagine.

He said, "If you will excuse me, I have a letter. I will see you after you have eaten perhaps?"

I said, "Fine."

I caught a signal from him to Johnny.

Johnny said to Liza, "I'll just wash up and be right with you."

He went into Friday's room with him and shut the door.

Liza said, "I'll get the stew. I put it on to reheat when I heard you come. He didn't ask if you wanted to wash too?"

"I'm fine, thanks," I said.

I waited while she went in the kitchen. Then I crossed

152

quickly to the door of Friday's room and put my ear to it.

I caught Johnny's voice saying, "But why the lake?"

Friday said, "Fool! Can't you see? It's the ideal place. Well hidden. Private —"

Liza was coming back with the stew from the kitchen so I could not listen any more. I slipped quickly back to the table as she came in. She put the stew on the table and began to serve it.

She said, "Wasn't Steve out of this world?"

I said, "Yes. Funny thing that. When Janie first met him she didn't like him a bit, remember?"

She gave me my plate.

"That's just it. From then on he set out to win her. I believe it was a challenge to him." She put her elbows on the table, a faraway look in her eyes. "You know, Sam, until tonight I haven't felt entirely happy about Steve. He's been so strange, it's been so difficult for me to know how to bridge the awful gap between us. You see, I was only four when I last saw him. Since he's been here he's hardly been out of his room or the study except to be with Johnny. But now, tonight, the way he couldn't stand the children not liking him, he's come out of his shell, agreeing to come riding with us all and everything. He's more like the old human Steve that I remember."

I wanted to tell her it was just an act so as to see the lake. I wanted to tell her so badly. But I knew I could not. I remembered what Mason Brown said. The U.S.A. came before Liza Oakes. She could not keep that secret. She would want to kill Johnny for that. I went on eating my stew.

I said, "Tell me, Liza, what does he do, Steve?"

"Do?"

"You say he's always in his room or in the study instead of helping you on the ranch."

"After all, Sam, he's only been here ten days. He's got to have time to settle down."

"I didn't mean any criticism, dear. Just wondered how he spent his time. You'd think he'd get kind of bored, just sitting."

"Oh, he writes letters."

"I shouldn't have thought he'd know anyone to write to in this country."

She said, "That's just what I asked him one day. And it's pathetic, Sam. He said he has a whole list of relatives of fellow prisoners. You see, the last few years he was in a camp there. And he promised them that if he got here he would write to all the relatives that they're still alive and how they are and so on. I think he feels very deeply about it all. Who wouldn't in his shoes?"

"I see. May I have a little more coffee?"

She poured it.

"I wonder what's keeping Johnny," she said. "I'll have to heat up the stew all over if he doesn't come soon. He's always been bad about meals."

"You and Johnny are truly happy, aren't you, dear?"

She looked at me and put her hand out and touched mine.

"I do believe that's what you came to see, isn't it? Well, it couldn't be better, I don't think."

"You don't think?"

She was looking at the flowers on the table center.

"I mean, I suppose men never love the way women do, really. It wouldn't be biological, would it?" She looked back at me and laughed. "Of course everything's all right, Sam. I think I'm a very lucky girl. Come on, let's not wait for him. He's in Steve's room. Listen to them yakking."

"Yakking, what a word." I got up after her. "Good thing he and Steve get on so well, isn't it?"

154

"Johnny's really wonderful about that, Sam. You know, I felt a little badly for his sake when I heard from Steve, I mean, having to have what almost amounts to a stranger staying in the house. It isn't as if we've been married for twenty years either. But Johnny puts himself out to be nice to him." She laughed. "Almost too much, sometimes. Want to say good night to the horses?"

"In the dark? You and horses — still the same, huh? We'll see them in the morning. I ought to go to Alice I think, pretty soon. But I know what I would like to see again, if you still have them."

"What?"

"Those soldiers. They were in the study, remember? You still have them?"

She smiled.

"Come on. I remember you two together over them so well. It seems like only yesterday. We'll go see. I don't think Johnny likes me to go in there too well, but what the heck."

"It's your study."

She looked at me.

"No, Sam," she said quietly. "I believe what Johnny believes. A wife is a wife. I have my job. The study is Johnny's."

"How about Steve, then?"

"Oh, he lets Steve use it to write in, that's all."

"That's nice," I said. "It's okay for Steve to use it, but not you."

We were crossing the living room and came to the door of the study. It was ajar. She pushed it open, and my eyes went immediately to the desk. There was nothing on it. Except a blotter. It was a big blotter, the good, solid, old-fashioned kind, with plenty of thick sheets. And there was writing on the top sheet. Plenty of writing on it.

Liza was looking at me and I saw she was hurt.

She said, "You still don't like Johnny, do you?"

"Is it surprising?"

Her head went back a little. There was that haughtiness back in her face now, her old spirit that even Johnny could not yet kill. And now it was being used in his defense. The desk lamp had been left turned on and it had a red shade and in the light from it shining on her hair and her upturned face, as she stood facing me, I could see quite well how beautiful she was.

Her beauty had in it now a mature quality that it had not had before when she was a girl; and if it seemed to contain tragedy that added to its classic quality I could not be sure whether this was due to my own imagination, in view of what I knew would be the doom of her happiness, or whether it was the way she was standing or whether it was the effect of the bathing of that face in the soft red light.

She said, "You have no right, Sam, to be like this with me. Once, perhaps, you might have taken the right, but you did not wish to. Don't you think you'd best take Alice away and leave us?"

I felt a lump in my throat. I wanted so badly to reach out with my hand and my voice and try to warn her, but I knew that I was helpless. And now I realized also that what she had just said was true, that I could have made things different for her if I had wanted to. There was nothing for me to say except what I said.

"I'm sorry, Liza dear. We'll go tomorrow afternoon, of course. But please let's part friends, you and I."

She smiled instantly.

"Of course," she said. She turned and went over to the cabinet in the corner.

While her back was turned I just had time to reach with

156

both hands on to the desk and jerk out the top sheet of the blotter and fold it and put it in my pocket. As I joined her at the cabinet I felt that I was the traitor. It was the same cabinet that was still there.

Liza opened the drawer.

"Come and see, they're still here, just the same as ever."

I went and stood by her, and together we looked at the forest of the little men in their wonderful array of uniforms, the little men who all had the same face. It was as if the old man was alive again and standing with us in the room. And I could hear his voice saying, "You see, put a man in uniform and you take away his face."

Liza said, "I think I was always a little jealous of them. There was something not quite right about his making them, I don't know what, though."

I became aware of a little sound behind us and turned and saw that Johnny was standing in the doorway.

He said, "I know exactly."

I heard Liza catch her breath. She was looking at Johnny. He was looking at her. They were locked. I might have been in the moon. There was something in the way they looked at each other that was as old and deep as a Scottish loch. You could not describe it. It was not love. It was not hate. It was not understanding. It was not misunderstanding. It was all of them. All of them.

Johnny broke it with a light laugh.

He said, "I put the stew on to reheat. Steve and I were talking. Sorry not to have been with you for dinner."

"That's okay," I said. "Liza was just showing me around. I think I'll go see how Alice is if you don't mind and turn in early. We've had kind of a long day."

"You bet. See you in the morning."

Liza said, "Good night, Sam dear. We'll have a lovely ride tomorrow."

I laughed.

"If I don't fall off. Night."

Johnny showed me to the door.

"Kind of dark," he said. "Want a flashlight?"

"No, thanks. I'll be fine."

He laughed, that light meaningless laugh.

"Watch out for snakes."

He shut the door. For a moment I could not see anything. I groped along the path and found the wicket and went through it. As I walked down past the house toward the guest cottage my eyes became accustomed to the darkness.

There was a light on in the guest cottage. I could see it through the curtains. I opened the door and went in.

Alice was in one of the beds. The bedside light was on. She had put the children to bed in the other room and she was alone.

She was crying.

I shut the door and went over to the bed and sat down and put my arms around her.

"Hey, there, you, girl. Hey."

She put her arms around me and clung tight. Like a baby. Like a girl. Like a woman.

"I thought you would never come."

"I came as soon as I could, honey. What is it?"

"I'm scared. He gives me the creeps. That act he put on with Janie. He deliberately made up to her, took her in a corner and told her some story till he had her telling him the three bears. He doesn't give a darn for her really. It was just an act. I know it was."

She was shaking. It wasn't for herself. I knew that. It was for the children. I remembered when Pete was nearly hit by a truck outside the house. I remembered when Janie

158

had convulsions, when she was six months. And this was worse, the shaking.

I said, "Sure it was an act, baby. Because he'd just heard about the lake and he wants an excuse to come with us and inspect it. Wants to use it as a rendezvous. Maybe a seaplane base or something." I told her what I had heard. I said, "Maybe Janie did hurt his feelings too. Even a horror like that can have feelings. But he used it as a cover up. To come out of his shell and come with us. Don't you see?"

She felt better for that. The shaking had stopped now.

She said, "All the same, why can't we just leave first thing? Why should we hang around?"

"Mason Brown may want us to introduce him. I'll call him early if I get the chance."

"Sam, whatever he says I'm not staying after lunch. Even if he does want us to. I just can't take any more, Sam."

"It's a deal. Stop worrying, will you?"

She looked up at me. Her eyes were blue and wet. I kissed them.

She said, "Go see if they're all right, will you, dear?"

"Of course. I was going to anyway."

"They insisted on sleeping in the loft."

I nodded and went into the other room. A small red candle bulb had been left turned on by the fireplace at the foot of the ladder leading up to the big bed at the top. I crossed the long room on tiptoe until I could see the head of the bed. From below I could not see if they were in the bed or not. I started to climb the ladder. The step creaked and I stopped, but there was still no sound from the bed. Suddenly I felt my heart pounding and I climbed up three more steps quickly and looked at the bed.

They were both fast asleep in the bed. Janie was on the

far side with her head across the pillow, and Pete was lying on the near side with one arm outside the covers holding Janie. At I stood there looking at them he opened his eyes and saw me and quickly put his fingers to his lips.

He whispered to me, "She was dreaming about a sand castle. It was a nightmare I think."

I nodded and whispered, "Good night, son. Go back to sleep now."

He put his head down and his eyes closed almost immediately and he was asleep again. I crept back down the ladder and across the room.

Alice looked at me as I came back in.

"Are they all right?"

"Sound as a bell. Stop worrying, will you?"

She gave a little sigh. I undressed and got into my bed. It was the same bed I had slept in that other night, ten years before, when I had wakened to the sound of the stallion.

Alice turned out the light. We lay in the dark.

She said, "Did you say anything to Liza?"

"About Friday?"

"Yes."

"Of course not."

"I wonder what she will do when it breaks."

"That's what I've been wondering. You know, it's a funny thing."

"What?"

"I was thinking. If it hadn't been for you I might have married her that time. And now she wouldn't be in this jam."

"I know. She's still in love with you."

"What makes you think that?"

"I just feel it. Maybe she doesn't even know it. But I felt it."

"Poor kid."

"Well, she didn't have to marry him."

"You don't understand. She's under his thumb."

"She likes it."

"Alice! How like a woman about another. First you say she's in love with me and then she likes being with Johnny."

"That's right. She'd rather have had you. But since she can't, she likes what she's got. Because she has to like it. It's easier to live that way. She couldn't live with it if she stood out against it. No one can live with something they hate. You die inside. Either she would have to leave him altogether or like to live with him. She can't decide to live a certain life and hate living it at the same time."

"How do you know all this?"

"Because I'm a woman. I understand what she's doing. It's not my cup of tea, but I understand it."

"Well, I'm darned if I do."

"I hope you never will. Good night, Sam. You're all right."

"Thanks, Mother. Maybe I ought to beat you every Saturday night."

"Watch out for the skillet if you do."

"I'm stronger than you are."

"That's why you won't beat me, you dope."

"Don't be so darn sure. Even I can be provoked out of being a dope."

"Then you'd lose your job and we'd starve."

"What do you mean?"

"Only a dope of the right kind could hold down that job."

"It's a darn good job and you know it."

"That's what I mean. Good night, Sam, it's late."

"Nuts to you. Good night."

I went to sleep. When I awakened it was still black. I wondered why I was awake. Then I remembered the blotting paper. I got up quietly and felt around in the dark so as not to awaken Alice. I found the blotting paper in my coat pocket where I had put it. I took it out and went into the bathroom and closed the door quietly and turned on the light. I held up the blotter in front of the mirror. I could not read a single word.

The writing was too blurred and overlaid for anything to be legible at all. Even around the edges it was blurred. I turned out the light and went back into the bedroom and put the blotting paper back in my pocket and thought maybe the F.B.I. might be able to get something from it, but I did not see how. I got back into bed and went to sleep.

10

In the morning it was raining. I could hear it before I opened my eyes and I thought at once that that would kill the lake expedition and I would not have to spend a morning with Liza and Alice together. Alice was still sleeping and I drew the curtain aside by my bed and looked out. It was not a heavy rain at all, just a light shower, and a local one at that. Farther off, toward the mountains, the sky was light and clear, and the sun was rising so that the valley was bathed in pink, the part that lay out of the rain. It was a strange sight. I let the curtain fall back and got up quietly so as not to wake Alice and went into the children's room to get them up. They were not in the bed.

I ran down the ladder. Their clothes were stashed on a chair, their night clothes. Then I saw their suitcase was gone through like a hurricane, but I wasn't too sure what was missing. I wondered whether to tell Alice right away or whether to go outside and try to track them. I ran back in the bedroom and jumped in my jeans and shoes and a T shirt. Alice did not wake. Then I ran out into the rain. It was only a light rain and it was ceasing too.

I ran toward the house, stepping as lightly as I could. Halfway across I saw them in the stableyard, under the eaves of the loose boxes, wearing their blue jeans, standing one on each side of Friday, holding his hands and watching the men getting out the horses.

163

Johnny was busy by the shed with the Jaguar. He had the rumble open and he was carrying out a carton and putting it in the car. I could see that it was a carton of Max's soup. He looked up and saw me and waved. I waved back. Liza called to me from the house and I saw her standing in the kitchen doorway.

"Breakfast in a half hour okay?"

I felt like a fool. Everything was normal.

"Fine," I said. "I was wondering about the rain."

"It's just a light shower. There won't be any more to stop us."

"Fine. I'll get Alice up."

She went back into the kitchen. I started toward the guest cottage. Then I saw that Johnny was not looking, so I slipped around the rear of the hedge, doubled back to the house and went in through the French windows behind and picked up the telephone by the study. I got the operator and asked for long distance and gave Mason Brown's number in Los Angeles that he had given me for such an hour. From where I stood I could see through the front window and watch Johnny still by the car near the shed. He was closing the door of the shed and locking it.

The operator came on the line and said the circuit was full and she would call back in a few minutes. Johnny was closing the rumble of the car now. I told the operator to cancel the call altogether, but she had gone off the wire already. Johnny was starting toward the house now. I jiggled the receiver and got another operator. I told her to get the long-distance operator because I wished to cancel a call. Johnny was halfway to the house. I heard Liza's footsteps coming from the kitchen to the dining room.

The long-distance operator came on the line. I heard Liza putting something down on the table and returning to the kitchen. I told the operator to cancel the long-

164

distance call I had just made. She asked me which call. Johnny was almost to the door. I told the operator the number I had called and she said she would cancel it.

I put down the telephone and ducked behind the closet door between the living room and the dining room. I did not have time to go out through the French windows before he opened the front door. He came in and went by the closet and through the dining room into the kitchen. Both the doors were open and I could hear everything and smell bacon cooking.

He said, "Where's Sam?"

I heard a dish set down on the stove or a table.

Her voice sounded surprised.

She said, "He went back to the cottage, didn't he?"

Johnny said, "That's what I'm asking you. I didn't see him go."

"Well, he's not here if that's what you mean. What's gotten into you, Johnny?"

"What did he want?"

"Just to ask if the rain would change the plans. I told him No."

"What else did you talk about, you two?"

"Look, Johnny, what is this?"

"You know very well. Come here."

"I will not. You may be the boss in the bedroom but not in the kitchen."

There was a silence.

Then Liza's voice again, a little uncertain this time.

"Besides, I'm cooking the bacon."

"Come here."

There was another silence. Then Liza's footsteps, slowly moving. They came to a stop. There was another silence.

Liza said, "Didn't you put me through enough last

night? I told you all we said. I told you I didn't love him. What more can you want?"

"You said you told him you did."

"You're twisting it, Johnny. I said I might have done. I didn't even say it, only implied it."

"You're doing the twisting. Now you listen to me. I don't want any funny business today."

"He's leaving at lunchtime anyway."

"There's all morning. You and your lake and your painting. I know you."

"Johnny, you've changed. Just because he came. It was you who asked them in the first place anyway."

"And why did he come?"

"But he's in love with Alice, he always has been, Johnny. You don't need to be so jealous, dear, truly you don't. You know that, don't you, Johnny? Oh, Johnny, please don't change back, please don't."

"Change back? I'd hardly be jealous if I did that, would I? Don't you remember? Didn't I suggest him to you then? Didn't I?"

"All right, Johnny. Let me go now, will you?"

"I'm not touching you. I'm not forcing you, am I?"

"Tell me I can go, please."

"Just watch it this morning then, will you? No twosomes."

"All right, Johnny."

"Promise?"

"I promise. The bacon's all burned. I can smell it."

"Cook some more. There's plenty of bacon."

"Sometimes I think I could kill you, Johnny."

He laughed.

"Do you? Even if you could, what would you do then? What would you do, Liza? Even if I just died?"

There was a silence.

166

"Don't say that, Johnny. Oh, Johnny."

There was another silence. Then he said, "Want any help?"

She laughed, a little low laugh.

"Go away, Johnny. Skit, you."

Her footsteps crossed the kitchen again, swift ones. Johnny's came toward the door. He passed by the closet and went across to the front door and opened it and went out. I stayed in the closet until the door closed. I could smell the burning bacon and I felt like vomiting.

Then I got out of the closet and across to the French windows and ducked down through them and out the garden to the hedge. I went along the back of the hedge that ran along the edge of the garden to the cottage. I could see Johnny walking back toward the Jaguar, and the kids playing with Friday. The rain had stopped now and they were playing leapfrog in the stableyard. I got back to the cottage and in through the back way.

Alice was in the front room packing the suitcases. She was wearing her blue jeans and her French kid riding boots that I had given her one birthday and a plaid shirt with a blue scarf knotted around her throat and her eyes were very blue and very clear as she looked at me.

"How is Liza today?"

I looked at her.

"Fine. Breakfast ready when we are."

"You help cook it?"

"Don't be like that, hon. What's the matter?"

"Why didn't you waken me, any of you?"

"Oh, that. Why, the kids wanted to look at the horses. I thought I'd let you sleep, that's all. You think it was because I wanted to see Liza?"

"Well, I see you left them alone with Friday."

"They'll come to no harm. I tried to call Mason Brown

but I couldn't get through." I told her what happened and said, "It looks as though you were right in what you said last night."

"It certainly does, chum." She snapped shut the suitcases and said, "The sooner we get away from here the better pleased I shall be."

"Whatever you feel it's as well not to show it in front of the others. Just act normal."

Alice gave a short laugh.

"What's normal about any of it?"

I took the suitcases out to the car. It was no use talking while she was that way, part strung up, part upset about Liza. I wished we could be gone as much as she did. But I knew we could not change our arrangements or it would look suspicious.

At breakfast she was still the same inside. I could tell that, though she didn't show it to the others. I wondered how long it would last. I had not seen her with such a bad one since Tim Hornbeck, way back before we were married.

"A penny for your thoughts," Liza said.

She was sitting next me at the breakfast table and I realized that I had not spoken for some time. Alice was sitting opposite next to Johnny, and Steve was sitting between the two children, who were keeping up a running fire of questions which Friday was handling well. He really did seem to be enjoying himself. Alice and Johnny were discussing arrangements about the cars and the horses so Janie wouldn't have to ride too far.

I turned to Liza and answered her question.

"I was thinking about women," I said.

Her eyebrows went up in a little quirk.

"At breakfast?"

"Always think about women at breakfast. Starts the day off right."

I knew Alice and Johnny were both listening and pretending not to. You could tell by the social quality of the dialogue about the cars and the condition of the road up through the woods and so on.

Liza laughed. It was a low musical laugh, but it did not fool me and I doubt if it fooled Johnny either because there was a trace of strain in it. Her shiny dark hair was very carefully brushed and her small oval face was very carefully made up and she was gay in a red and brown spotted shirt, but there were those deep pools inside her eyes that made me think of the water she painted.

She said, "I guess the formula wouldn't work out for me." She turned to the others and said, "If we're all through we'd best get started. What did you arrange about the cars?"

Johnny said, "I take the Jag to the fork so Steve and I can go straight to the inn without coming back here. Alice says she'll take their car to the fork so that they can do the same and you can lead our spare horses up and meet us there."

Liza said, "How will the horses get back from the fork if we all go straight to the inn for lunch?"

"Have West meet them. We leave them tied there. He can bring them in."

"All right."

I said, "I'll take the car to the fork if you like, Alice."

"No thanks. You like riding better than I do. Besides, I can take Janie with me so she won't have so far to ride."

Janie started to scream.

"I want to ride all the way."

I said, "I can always take her on my horse with me any time she gets tired. It's not too far."

169

Friday said, "She can come on my horse some of the way."

Janie beamed.

Pete said, "That's sissy."

Alice said to me, "You make the arrangements, dear, and just let me know what they are."

We all got up on that and went outside.

11

It had stopped raining and the sky was as clear as a bell. You would not think it had known a cloud since the Stone Age. The horses were all waiting. Johnny climbed in the Jag and set off slowly up the gravel road. Alice followed in our car. I kept Janie with me and Pete. She was happy on a paint horse. Friday and Pete rode on each side of her. Liza and I followed, leading the spares. We rode up over the rolling ranch hills toward the edge of the woods that stretched to the tops of the mountains.

Liza and I did not talk much. It was so clearly a rare occasion, the first and, I thought, probably the last, that we should ever ride together. I had never seen her ride, just photographs. At once it somehow seemed familiar to me, the way she rode, as though I had known it all my life, like watching Pavlova dance or Tilden play tennis or any champion at his own. It was watching riding itself. There was never a moment when she was not right, and she never thought about it.

I wondered what she was thinking about, remembering what Alice had said last night, and what Liza had said too, and I could feel a bond between us as we rode up over the rolling hills toward the woods and the mountains. I wanted so much to tell her something, but Friday was always within earshot and all the time Mason Brown's words were in my ears; so I held my tongue and looked at

171

the country and saw first one painting of hers after another and pointed them out to her, and she smiled at me.

"Wait till you see the lake," she said.

Friday was doing fine with the children. Watching him I found it hard to believe he was anything but what he seemed, a man fond of children. Then I thought why should he not be for that matter? If I were a spy in Russia and I met some cute Russian kids I could be fond of them. Also what better way of camouflaging yourself than to be nice to everyone? If you were going to do something, especially spying, do it 100 per cent or not at all, because there will always be someone else who will beat you at it otherwise. And you can't afford to be beat in that game. An honest to God out and out spy had to be a very brave man because he was all on his own, completely, with no one to back him up if he failed, as he was almost bound to do in the end.

I began to feel almost sorry for Friday, to think that he had been spotted even before he reached the shore. And all the plans had been so carefully laid, his background so well established, so that he could sit in his spider's web and send out his correspondence and make a guest ranch up at the lake where he could arrange rendezvous, even build a radio station up there, maybe, and land planes on the lake. Whatever Friday had in mind, Mason Brown would be watching him, ready to pounce when he saw fit. I felt in my pocket for the piece of blotting paper. It was still there.

The fork lay just ahead of us now, and the cars were waiting. Alice and Johnny were standing together by the Jaguar. He had the hood open and he was showing her the motor. I knew she did not give a hoot about motors, but she was making like she was interested enough. The motor was running gently and he was pointing things out to her.

He walked back to the wheel and reached in his hand and opened the throttle to show her something while she was watching the engine. The motor roared. Friday's horse bucked and he fell off. Liza went white.

Johnny and Alice looked up and saw us and he switched off the motor. The kids' horses were quiet and I saw that they were all right. I looked at Liza again. She was looking at Friday and her face was still white. She did not say anything.

He remounted and Johnny and Alice got mounted and everyone was talking at once and we rode off up the dirt rode to the lake. Alice rode with the children and Friday, and Liza rode between Johnny and me. Her eyes were all the time on Friday now as he rode and her mouth was taut. I saw Johnny notice it too.

He said, "What's the matter, baby?"

We were riding through a glade in the woods halfway up the mountain now and the others were cantering ahead through the long grass.

Liza looked at Johnny.

She said, "That's not Steve."

I felt my heart pound. Johnny stared at her. His eyes flicked to me and back to her.

"What do you mean? Are you crazy?"

"The way he rides." She put out a hand on Johnny's rein, as though for support. "Johnny, he's an impostor, he must be. No one forgets how to ride."

I waited for Johnny to climb out of that one.

He was startled all right.

He said, "Was Steve a good rider?"

She said, "He taught me everything. He was wonderful. Johnny, it's — it's —" She couldn't go on.

Johnny said, "Take it easy. This is ridiculous. You were

only four. You can't remember properly. Everything seems wonderful then."

"Johnny, that's one thing I'm positive about. I don't remember him well. All right. But I do remember his riding."

There was a silence. We rode on. I thought fast and decided that to say nothing might make Johnny suspicious of me.

I said, "But Liza, why would he be an impostor? It doesn't make sense. He has to have his papers to be here anyway."

Johnny said, "All right, Liza, I'll have to tell you something." His voice sounded reassured, confident now. He said, "He didn't want you to know."

She looked at him.

"Know what?"

"His leg." He cupped his hands and called. "Steve!"

She was looking puzzled. I wondered how Johnny was going to get out of it. And Friday too. It was going to be something to see, this. I watched while Steve and the others stopped and looked back.

"What is it?" Friday called.

"Come here a minute."

The sunlight shone on his horse's white blaze as Friday cantered him back toward us. Alice and the children, after a brief pause, had continued on ahead. Liza was looking at Friday now as he rode up, looking from him to Johnny and back, inquiringly.

We had not stopped riding forward, at a walk, so that it was not long before the gap was closed between us and him. I kept my horse walking forward as though it were none of my business if they wanted to stop and talk or to do so in front of me if they wished. They kept going too.

"Can't it keep, Johnny? I was having fun."

174

Johnny said, "No, it can't keep, Steve. Liza thinks you're an impostor because you don't ride the way you did. I told her it was your leg and it was your secret, why you didn't ride any more, why you can't abide horses any more. Tell her, Steve. I knew you'd have to in the end. Tell her about your leg."

"My leg? You have told her?"

Liza was looking straight at Friday.

She said, "I don't care what you did to your leg. It still couldn't change a man from a great rider to a clumsy sot like you. Who are you anyway?"

Johnny said, "Liza, honey! You mustn't talk to Steve that way. It's not just his leg."

She turned to Johnny.

"Johnny, he deceived you all right because you didn't know Steve. But he can't deceive me. Not with that seat on a horse. I don't know why I didn't notice it right away. I knew there was something strange, but I guess I just didn't think what it was, not until he fell off."

She was scornful. To her you could see that this thing was something to scorn, not something to fear. I felt glad for her, but I felt afraid for her too and I thought fast as to what course of action I should take if anything drastic were to happen.

Johnny turned on Friday.

"You had better explain yourself, mister," he said. "You heard what my wife just said."

I watched Friday's face. It was something to see, the way he handled it. In that moment, right away, I knew he was tops by the way he handled it.

He stopped his horse and we all stopped with him. He did not look at Johnny. He just sat there on his horse and looked at Liza. And somehow, without a muscle of his face moving, his eyes moistened, watered, and teardrops

175

actually rolled down his cheeks. When he spoke his voice was barely steady, as though fighting for control of himself.

"Do you remember Sandy, Liza?"

She was staring at him and staring at him. You could see that she did not know what to think now.

She said, not taking her eyes off Friday's face, "Johnny, did you ever tell him about Sandy?"

Johnny said, "Sandy? Who's he?"

She looked at Johnny.

"You know, Johnny, I told you about Sandy. The cocker?"

"Oh, you mean the one in the picture you have?"

"You didn't tell him anything about Sandy, did you, Johnny?"

"No. Tell the truth, I'd even forgotten his name was Sandy till you mentioned it this minute. No, of course I didn't tell him."

She turned back to Friday.

"Well?"

"Do you remember, the day I went away, the last time you ever saw me, do you remember I gave Sandy to you and you said, 'No, he's your dog, he'll pine away. You must take him with you.' And I told you I was going on a boat and you were to take care of Sandy for me and I would take him back when I got back, if you wanted me to. Do you remember that?"

She nodded, her eyes fast on his face.

"What happened to Sandy, Liza?" he asked suddenly.

"He — he died, he pined away just like I said, when you didn't come back — but it doesn't make sense. How could you possibly have forgotten how to ride? It doesn't make sense."

The tears began to roll again now. He had turned them off earlier, but now he had them going again.

He said quietly, "You don't know much about fear, do you, Liza?"

"Fear?"

He nodded. He waited longer this time before he spoke. His timing was terrific.

He said, "It was in the desert, crossing Arabia, that caravan. About six weeks after the shipwreck. We slept hidden by day, traveled by night. And you couldn't drop out of that caravan. No one could drop out of that caravan. It wasn't physically possible. And then I got gangrene in my leg, from the wound when I fought the dhow captain, coming across the Red Sea. I knew it was the end. Gangrene always was in those days. I wanted to be left to die. But they wouldn't leave me. Know what they did? They put me on a horse. On a horse with that rotting leg. They tied some filthy earth mold around my leg and put me on that horse. On we went. On and on through the desert. Every step was agony. Every step. I tried to throw myself off. They held me on. I hated them. But I hated the horse most. All that pain I associated with the horse. Ever since then, deep inside of me, my one great enemy, my one great fear, was a horse. Any horse. I'll never ride as I used to, Liza. Never again. Two reasons. The fear, and the leg. It will never be right again, that leg, never."

Liza was trembling a little now as she sat on her horse. I could see that she was trembling a little. He had sold her. It was like taking candy from a baby. And all he had to start with, all Johnny had thrown him, was a leg and a hatred of horses.

I thought I had better take an intelligent interest.

I said, "But what happened about the gangrene? How could you possibly have survived it?"

177

He looked at me.

He said, "That was what I thought at the time. How could I possibly survive? That was what made my fear a thousand times worse, the certainty I was going to die. But there was one thing I didn't know. Had I known it, had they told me, maybe I wouldn't have had the terrible fear."

He stopped. We all waited for him to go on.

Liza said, "What was that?"

He turned back to me.

"How do they cure gangrene nowadays?"

"Penicillin," I said.

"And what is penicillin?"

"It's a mold."

He nodded.

"Exactly. That's what they used on me. A mold. I've no explanation. Except that they must have known the secret, maybe centuries before we did."

I nodded convincingly to him. I had fallen right into it. He had planted that mold early on and he must have had it figured about the penicillin. Of course it was non-sense. But it sounded good enough for any layman.

It was good enough for Liza. She was crying now. She rode up to Friday and put a hand on his arm. For a moment I thought she was going to kiss him. I wanted to shout, but I had to keep my face right.

Liza said, "Steve, I'm sorry, dear. You shouldn't have come this morning."

"It's good for me," he said. "And I do want to see the lake."

I thought, you sure do, chum.

Liza smiled at him through her tears.

"You want to be with the children. And I stopped you. I'm sorry, Steve. Go ahead."

He smiled at her, patted her hand, wheeled his horse and rode off, riding in his own clumsy fashion. Looking at him you could almost believe now that there rode a man who, but for the grace of God and a bad leg, might have been a wonderful rider, perhaps once was. The power of the spell was like that. I saw Liza's eyes, still tear stained, following him as he rode up the trail road, and I knew she was thinking that way.

"I warned you, Liza," Johnny said.

"I'm sorry, Johnny. Why didn't you tell me?"

"It was his secret. His feelings."

"I wish I had bitten my tongue out."

"Come on." Johnny spurred his horse. "Let's go."

There was a ring to his voice now, and I knew that Liza was somehow more in his power than ever. I cursed Mason Brown and the whole situation as we rode on up the trail behind Johnny. But I knew I could do nothing.

We topped the rise ahead and there was the lake. There was the lake, exactly and identically as it was in the painting that had hung the last ten years over our bed. It was the strangest sensation you can imagine, suddenly coming on a familiar sight like that in such a completely unexpected way.

Instinctively I stopped my horse. And Liza stopped beside me, and I knew she was looking at me as I looked at the lake. Johnny was riding on ahead and for a moment we were alone together.

"It's fantastic," I said. "Except that it's larger than the painting makes it, that's the only difference. Especially today, all the lighting is the same, even the reflection of the far hills."

She said, "I wanted to see you see it from this spot. From here is my favorite angle. You get the best proportion of incident, foreground and background, and with that contrast of light, water and sky. But I do tend to make it look smaller than it really is. It's all of four miles across!"

"The country's big in proportion," I said. "I wouldn't worry about it if I could paint the way you can, no sir."

She smiled with pleasure.

"Thank you, Sam."

Johnny was almost by the boathouse now, where the others had dismounted and tied the horses, when he turned and saw that we had not followed.

"Oh, Liza," he called.

She said, "Let's go, Sam."

We rode forward. She seemed to feel guilty. A twosome. Well, it had been a very short and innocent one.

"What is it, Johnny?" she asked as we rode up.

His eyes were broody.

He said, "I clean forgot till this minute. Robbie phoned about Black Susan. He's coming this morning."

"Johnny! What time?"

"He just said before lunch."

"Why didn't you tell me?"

"It was yesterday afternoon, just before these people came. I'm sorry dear, I forgot till this second. Maybe West can take care of it."

"You know he can't."

She turned to us.

"I've got to go back. Man about a horse. I'll meet you at the inn."

I felt darn sure he had just invented it to punish her for her twosome.

I said, "We might as well all go then. Now that we've seen the lake."

Alice said, "I think the children would be disappointed, Sam. We've come to teach them fishing, so we should do

180

it." She stamped out a cigarette with her boot and turned and called to the boathouse.

"Children, what are you doing?"

Friday and Pete came out of the boathouse. Pete was bug-eyed. But before he could speak Janie rushed out and ran to Alice smiling like a devil.

"I had to go, so I went in the boat, Mamma."

"Janie!"

She started jumping up and down and laughing at Alice.

"It's got a toilet, you see, a real toilet."

Alice said, "All right, but don't point your finger at me. It's rude."

Pete said, "It's not just a speedboat, it's a little cruiser. It's got a bell on it yet. It will go —" he turned to Friday, "how many knots did you say?"

Friday was looking at the lake, studying it.

He turned to Pete.

"I guessed forty, is that right, Johnny?"

"About that," Johnny said.

Pete said, "Can we go in it now?"

I said, "No, son, first we're going fishing, remember?"

I turned to Liza.

"It's a darn shame you have to go. We'll see you at lunch then?"

She smiled.

"Of course." She looked at Alice. "I do hope you understand. If this husband of mine didn't have a sieve for a memory —" She broke off with a little laugh.

Alice smiled at her.

"I understand perfectly," she said. "We'll be fine."

Liza said, "See you at the inn then." She turned her horse and cantered evenly along the uneven track and disappeared among the trees.

I got off my horse and tied him up and said, "Let's get the fishing boat ready. How about bait, Johnny?"

"Bait? Aren't you going to troll? That's the best way here. Troll in the middle of the lake." We were all walking to the boathouse now. Johnny was saying, "Last year Liza and I caught some beauties that way." He stopped and pointed across the lake. "See that tip of the shore directly across, the one with the jutting rock and the big live oak? Aim for that and start trolling about a mile and a half from here. It's a long pull, but it's worth it. For that matter you can have your lines out from the start, but I'll take a bet you won't get anything till you're about halfway across the lake. Not at this time of day, in the fall."

"Okay," I said. "It's quite a row though."

"Oh, you can take turns. Steve or I would help row but the boat's not big enough for one thing, and we've got to fix the cruiser ready for when you get back. You can use the outboard to come back on when you're through fishing so you won't have to row back."

"Well, glad to hear you have one. That's something."

I saw he was right, the boat wasn't big enough for more than the four of us fishing. It was a small rowboat with an outboard motor on the stern. Johnny got the rods and we began to fix the leaders and the spoons while the kids crowded round asking questions all the time. Alice wasn't saying much. She just quietly helped with the tackle. Friday was going over the cruiser. She was a beauty all right, like Pete said, a twenty-seven footer, Chris-Craft.

We got the lines all set and into the boat and got in the boat and started out. I took the oars and Alice and the kids distributed themselves with the four lines. They paid out the lines after I had rowed a little way out. There was hardly a ripple on the water.

182

12

I could see Friday and Johnny clambering around the cruiser as I rowed, getting it ready. They got gradually smaller as I rowed on. It was hot, rowing without any wind, and I paused to take off my coat. The children's lines ran afoul of each other and Alice had to untangle them, and referee the quarrel as to whose fault it was. We were getting near to the center of the lake now. An airliner flew overhead, maybe another three thousand feet higher than we were, en route to San Francisco.

I thought if Friday was planning to use the lake as a seaplane rendezvous he would have to watch for that. There wasn't much cover from being seen by one of the airline pilots. Though if they did see a seaplane on the lake they might not think anything of it. But if there was cover it would eliminate the risk. There were overhanging trees at the south end of the lake. Maybe that was what Friday had been looking for when he was studying the lake. And then I thought anything to do with seaplanes was unlikely. Who would use such things these days anyway?

Alice said, "What was he called back for? What took so long?"

It was the first time she had spoken.

The kids were quarreling again and not listening.

I said, "Liza thought he was an impostor. Because he

183

couldn't ride like Steve. He got out of it. You should have seen. It was something."

She looked scared.

"You didn't give away anything?"

"No, Alice. I did not."

I turned to look at the lines. Pete's was jumping. He was not paying attention. He was lecturing Janie. He was saying, "You shouldn't have even one secret with a strange man, you know that."

I said, "Quick, Pete boy, you've got a bite. Do what I told you."

He got all excited, forgot his lecture, grabbed his rod. He made the strike all right. The fish held. He began to play it.

"Easy now," I said. "You're doing fine. Keep it taut. Even pressure on him. That's a boy. What's this about secrets, anyway?"

His eyes were sparkling. He was like someone playing a violin. His whole being was in it. It was his first fish.

He said, "Oh, just Janie and Uncle Steve have a secret. Dad, now I should reel in more, shouldn't I? Now?"

"If it feels easy. That's right. What secret was it, do you know?"

"She won't tell. Please, Dad, I'm concentrating."

I looked at Alice. She was looking at me. We looked at Janie. She was watching Pete's line.

Alice said, "What was the secret with Uncle Steve, Janie?"

Janie said, "I want to catch the fish."

Alice said, "Yes, darling, but what was the secret?"

"I promised not to tell."

"You mustn't promise strangers. You know that. What was it, Janie? Mamma has to know."

"Can I hold Pete's line if I tell?"

184

I said, "Yes, Janie, you can."

Pete said, "She cannot hold my line. Dad!"

I said, "What was it, Janie?"

She said, "He trod on my sand castle. But he was nice so I forgave him and promised not to tell. Now can I hold the line?"

She made a grab for the line. Pete slapped her. The line went slack.

"Now you've lost my fish! My first fish!"

Janie began to cry. Alice sat her on her lap. "Do you mean he trod on your sand castle that day we were on the beach. When Dad and I were swimming? Is that when you mean?"

She was still crying a little, but she stopped and said, "Yes, he came out of the water and trod in it."

Pete said, "I didn't see him. She's making it up. Why did you let her lose my fish, Dad? My first fish?"

Janie said, "You weren't watching. You were looking at Dad and Mamma in the sea."

So Friday had not recognized Alice. But he had recognized Janie, and, worse still, she had recognized him. . . .

Across the lake I heard the roar of the motor of the speedboat. I looked toward the boathouse. The cruiser was just leaving. It was headed straight toward us. And we were in the middle of the lake.

They had a twenty-seven foot cruiser. We had a small wooden rowboat. And if it was rammed it could not float because of the outboard motor. The outboard motor would take it down. There would be nothing to float on. And it was a two mile swim either way. And they could circle around us till we drowned. Family drowns in lake. Tragic accident. How simple it was. How simple I was. Seaplanes . . .

We had two minutes left. Maybe two and a half. Alice

185

was looking at me. She read it all. For a moment there was panic in those blue eyes.

I said, "Steady, chum. Try the motor."

She was in the stern, right next to it. She tried it. It was dead.

"No gas," she said.

Pete said, "Why are they coming so soon? They'll disturb the fish."

Janie said, "My good! It goes a hundred twenty-six I think. Let's go in it. Are they coming for us to go in it?"

I said, "Now I've got a secret to tell you. All of you. We're going to play a new game. Uncle Steve and Uncle Johnny and I invented it this morning. First they have the speedboat and we have the rowboat. Then we have the speedboat and they have the rowboat. They won the speedboat first. The game is for the speedboat to try and sink the rowboat. Then the people in the rowboat, that's us, pretend to drown. Whoever stays under the water longest is judged the winner."

I looked into Alice's blue eyes.

"And they don't know we are a swimming family. So we'll fool them easily if we remember our underwater swimming. Remember, everybody, to take a deep breath before you dive under. Now, off with our boots, everyone. Quick. Jump to it."

The cruiser was almost halfway. Janie was fooled. Alice blinked her approval. Pete was puzzled.

"But, Dad, why — ?"

Alice cut him short.

"Come on, Pete, off with those boots."

She started to take Janie's off. I leaned forward and helped Pete with his. I thought, thank God for good old-fashioned training in obedience.

I took Alice's left foot and ripped off her boot. The

186

French kid made it easy. She said, "Sam, take your own off. Quick."

Mine were not French kid. The cruiser had reached the halfway mark now. She was doing all of forty knots. Her bow was way up, half the boat was out of the water. It was a beautiful sight, the cleavage of the water, the great banks of white on either side, shaped like a darting arrow, darting straight for us. I took it all in in a tenth of a second. Then I was back at my boot, wriggling my heel back and forth, back and forth. The leather was stiff. The others had theirs off now. My heel came free at last. I had one boot off. I started on the other heel.

I said, "Now everybody unbutton your shirts and jeans, but don't take them off till we get underwater. We're going to fool them that we're surprised."

I was busy with my right heel. It was slowly, slowly, beginning to work upwards, a little with each sideways movement.

Pete said, "But they know we know about the game, so how can it be a surprise? You mean we're going to cheat a little, maybe?"

I looked up at him and winked.

"Maybe," I said.

He grinned and started to unbutton his clothes. Alice was wonderful. After the first panic she had steadied completely. It was the kids' being there that forced it. There was no alternative but to stay steady. I wondered how it would have been, Alice and I alone together. It would have been harder for her. She would not have been a mother at bay. In that moment, as my right heel was slowly working loose, and the kids and Alice were unbuttoning their shirts and loosening their belts, and the sun was beating down hot on my back, and the roar of the motor was coming closer and closer, in that moment I was proud that we were a family, a complete family, all together, and ready for our drowning.

The pulsation of the motor dropped suddenly. I looked up at the speedboat. She was close now, and only on quarter speed. Maybe fifteen knots. Then I saw why. Now her bow had dropped into the water. That way she could ram us. They had tied some gunny sacking over the bow. That way there would not be any evidence of our boat slivers in her.

They had thought of everything, from sending Liza down the hill, to keeping Janie's mouth shut, to getting us in the middle of the lake with our boots on, to the gunny sacking. They could say at lunch they left because we wanted to continue fishing awhile. Then we wouldn't be at lunch. Maybe we had said we were going right on to San Luis Obispo. Maybe, later on, after the speedboat's bow was repaired, an accident would be discovered. Our bodies might float. But not the rammed boat. It would be at the bottom of the mountain lake, and mountain lakes were deep, too deep to dredge, deep and cold. . . .

I could see Johnny at the wheel now. And Friday was standing beside him. He was smoking a cigarette. They were closing in fast. I looked around. We were closer to the far side than the boathouse, if anything.

I said, "Listen everyone. We're going to swim underwater. Aim for the rocky point on the far side. Stay underwater. When you come up for air, only put your mouths up. Don't let them see or hear you. Start swimming directly you go under. That way we'll fool them. They'll be watching here. Alice, take Janie. Pete with me. Ready?"

Pete said, "But, Dad, we can't swim that far."

I said, "It's just an aiming point for the game, you dope. To keep us together."

Janie chuckled.

188

"You dope! Pete's such a dope, isn't he?"

Alice took her hand, looked at me over her head. Her eyes were steady now. We smiled at each other. We knew what it meant. Thank you for a lifetime. Just in case . . .

I stood up, waved at the cruiser, cupped my hands.

"Hey, you're going to ram us! Watch out!"

It was for show.

Fifteen feet, ten feet.

"Take a deep breath everyone. Jump!"

Alice jumped with Janie off the stern. I took Pete from the bow. The cruiser hit in the middle of the boat. We were underwater.

The water was cold. Then the first shock was over. I held my breath. I looked at Pete. No bubbles from him so he was holding his. He was watching me. I let go his hand and started swimming down deep. He came alongside. I straightened out. We had gone under the cruiser. That was something Alice and Janie would not have to do because they were on the right side already. I could feel the propeller's vibrations through the water. It seemed as if they were backing up after the ram. They would be watching for us now, sitting up there on the bridge watching for us to come up and splash around and scream. If we didn't come up they would figure we had drowned with our boots on. They didn't know we could swim. Except Johnny knew that I could, that was all. They had not seen Alice in the sea that day, and Johnny knew I had heavy boots on.

We swam on, breast stroke. Pete was a beautiful swimmer. And he could hold his breath longer than I could. I was beginning to feel it now. But I could hear the motor vibrations increasing. They must be circling. Then I realized the vibrations were not growing. They were faster, yes, but they were going away from us. They must be circling the other way. I had to come up. Pete came up with me. I looked up, trying to see the surface. I didn't want to break it with my hands.

Suddenly I saw it. I backed my stroke, put up my mouth. I could not watch Pete now. I broke surface with my face, took a deep breath. The air was wonderful, wonderful, wonderful. I backed down again quick. I did not dare take time to look. When I got down six feet I turned over and started swimming again and bumped someone. It was Pete. He was swimming at an angle. I pointed ahead, what I thought was the direction. I was pretty sure it was the direction, though I could not be quite sure because I had not had time to check. He changed direction, swam on beside me.

I wondered about Alice and Janie. I wondered if Johnny and Friday could possibly have missed seeing any of us. But now I could not hear or feel the motor vibrations any more. They must have been circling the other way when we came up. Maybe we had been lucky. We surely deserved to be lucky. Surely we deserved to be lucky. All the years of swimming we had done. Pete could swim when he was two. Janie could swim before she could walk. I thought of Janie's little tiny baby's body swimming like a tadpole in the big pool in Westwood. How she cried and cried when Alice took her out of the water. When she was eighteen months she would bring a little bucket off the bottom. It was a little red bucket. She slept with it under her pillow. It made the pillow uncomfortable, but she would not go to sleep if it was not there. Then she would sleep with her head askew and her mouth open. Alice said she would grow up with a permanent crick in her neck. Alice said she would change into a frog in the night, one night. Alice used to laugh and say — used to? Used to, hell. Alice was not dead. Nobody was dead. Pete was pull-

190

ing at my arm. He pointed up. We came up together. I had stayed longer than I should this time. Even Pete needed air. I had stayed too long. I wanted to burst upwards. I held it and held it. Just a little longer. Then I saw the light, opaque light, but light. I held it in and backed. Slowly my face broke.

I gulped it. This time I took two gulps of it. And my whole face had come out. I opened my eyes. My ears came out. I heard the roar of the motor. It was going full speed. I looked. I saw it. It was going full speed. It was going full speed straight back to the boathouse.

Pete breathed heavily.

"Dad! They're leaving us!"

"Trust me, son. Down, quick, and strip underwater."

"Yes, Dad. I trust you, Dad."

We went down again. We struggled out of our shirts and jeans. Almost at once we had to come up again. The boat was nearly back to the boathouse now. There was no sign of our boat. And there was no sign of Alice and Janie. There was no sign at all.

I knew there was nothing to do. If they were gone, they were gone. To stay up was dangerous in either case. It was endangering Pete for sure. And if they weren't gone, it was endangering them too.

Down we went again. We swam on. It was easier now. The jeans had got waterlogged and it was wonderful to be rid of them. It was like a second lease on life. I had not dared strip before they were waterlogged in case they had surfaced and given us away. But now they sank. In the end everything sank. In the end. And then, when bodies were bloated again after death they came up and floated. Women floated up and men floated down. Or was it the other way round? Which way did children float?

We came up again. The motor had ceased. The cruiser

had reached the boathouse. I could see the outline of the cruiser against the boathouse, slowly moving in. And silhouetted against it also, just twenty-five or thirty yards behind us, was Alice's head and Janie's head. A five-year-old can be a good swimmer. But not as fast as an eight-year-old. Not so fast, but as good. . . .

I saw Pete was going to wave and shout to them.

"No, Pete, no. Don't move your arms and don't shout. Stay still and float. We'll wait for them."

"Yes, Dad." He did as I told him. He was looking at me. He said, "It isn't really a game at all, is it, Dad?"

I said, "No, son, it isn't. But we mustn't let Janie know. As long as she doesn't know she will be all right. We're going to make it all right, son."

He did not answer that. I looked round. I could see that our heads were directly in line between the boathouse and the rocky point. The rocky point was dark-colored, so there was an excellent chance that our heads would not show up to Johnny and Friday as long as they were at water level. But when they started to ride away and got up the hill a bit toward the rise, then they might see them against the background of the lake water.

Pete said, "Why do they want to drown us?"

"Because they are Russian spies and know we found out about them."

"Gee!"

"Let's save breath, son. Long way to go."

"Yes, Dad. But, can we make it, you think?"

"Why not? We've got all day. Float when we tire. Easy."

"Mom or Janie may get cramps."

Or Dad or Pete or all four of us. It was cold enough. But it could have been colder.

I said, "We never get cramps in our family. Feel cold?"

"No, Dad. Not yet."

I wondered what to do. Whether to send him off swimming again or wait a little longer. Alice and Janie were closing up now. She had evidently figured as I had and decided to stay on the surface. They were keeping their arms and legs underwater, just their heads were bobbing toward us. I decided to wait.

While waiting I took another look toward the boathouse. Being over two miles away everything was very small. But I could see moving figures. And I could tell which was which, too, because Johnny had on a blue shirt and Friday had on a black and white check. And they were both leaving the boathouse now, as I watched, and walking away, presumably toward the horses. I could not see the place where we had tied the horses because of the terrain. There was a dip and some rocks and some trees right there. But somehow I got the impression, the way those two figures were moving away from the boathouse, that they were going direct to the horses, men about their business, with no further worries about a family that had disappeared beneath the center of a four mile wide lake with their boots on. Perhaps it was the pace at which they moved, those figures. There was nothing casual about it. In fact they seemed to be moving in quite a hurry to get gone.

Alice and Janie had reached us now. They too had stripped their shirts and jeans. I looked at them anxiously. Alice looked all right, but Janie's body looked cold. Alice was looking at Pete and me to see if we were all right.

She smiled at me. I smiled back at her. She said, "You shouldn't have waited, Sam. You've got to get Pete in."

Pete said, "I'm fine, Mom. Don't you worry over me."

Janie said, "I won. But I lost my new belt. Daddy,

193

Mamma promised me a new belt if I won. She wouldn't let me dive for my belt. It had a silver buckle."

Pete said, "What do you need a belt for, stupid? You've got no pants anyway."

Janie said, "I will have pants. New ones. Mamma said so. And I won. I stayed under longest. Why don't they come back now I won?"

Alice said, "They will, honey. Meanwhile we'll all swim ashore and surprise them. The game is to reach the shore before they reach us. If we can do that we get a speedboat for a prize, don't we, Sam?"

"That's right," I said. "A brand new speedboat just for us. Come on, let's go. Unless you want a rest, Alice?"

"I'm fine." She looked at Janie. "How do you feel, honey?"

"I want a saver."

I said, "All right, I'll give you one. Alice, you go with Pete."

I took a look back at the far shore again. Now I could see two horses being ridden up the slope to the trees. They were not looking back. But they might. If they did, it would be just too bad. I did not dare have Janie go under again. Or any of us for that matter. We had little enough to spare for that swim as it was.

I said, "Hold still everyone till I give the word to swim. Float quietly now."

Pete was watching them too. They disappeared among the trees and he looked at me. He was scared.

I said, "We'll make it easy now. Swim any way you want to now."

Pete said in a low voice, "Take care of Janie, Dad. She can't make it alone."

"Don't worry, son. We'll all make it easy. No strain at all."

194

He made a light come into his eyes and smiled a little.

"You bet, Dad."

"Come, Janie," I said.

Alice said, "I'll spell you later."

"You bet," I said.

We all started swimming. I swam on my back, holding Janie's head and swimming just with my legs. Alice and Pete began to draw away a little, swimming a sidestroke, keeping a steady rhythm. The sun was high now. It must have been around noon. We would be ashore before it lost its power too much. Unless we got cramps first. Even if one of us got cramps, what then?

What then?

I decided to put it out of my head. It was a negative thought. Negative thoughts were no good. Positive thoughts were good. I thought about God. I looked up at the sky and thought about God. God's in His heaven and all's right with the world.

Janie said, "I don't want a speedboat. I wish they'd come."

I began to feel my lung. I had not felt my lung for five years. I decided it was nerves. It didn't make sense to feel it otherwise. I had swum plenty in the last five years and I had never felt my lung.

I said, "Of course you want a speedboat. It's not just for you. It's for all of us. Mamma and Pete and me too. You can be the captain and walk on the bridge and ring the bell."

"Can I have a new cap?"

"Yes."

"And a new belt? I want a new belt."

"Of course."

"Why don't they come? I want Mamma."

So do I. So do I. I must have stayed under too long that

time. It was no good this. It was no good at all. Breathing. Like the oxygen going off at thirty thousand. I turned my head and looked for Alice and Pete, to see how far on they had got. They were twenty yards to the good. The rocky point looked just as far away as ever. Maybe we had covered a hundred and some since the boat sank. But what was that in two miles?

Well, all right, what was it? A hundred fifty yards, let us say, out of twice seventeen hundred fifty-six. That was around a twentieth. Nineteen more rounds to go. With a five-year-old and an eight-year-old and a bad lung. And Alice not in training. Maybe Alice alone could make it. Maybe Alice and Pete could make it, resting him often. But not Janie. If I got her on my back? My legs were beginning to rebel against the present stroke anyway. I decided I would turn on my side and put Janie straddling my waist. That was what I would do. That should help the breathing too, just to change position. I started to turn over, at the same time pulling Janie up to my waist. Then I started to cough.

My head went under and I had to let Janie go. Fortunately I had air in when it went under, but some water went in too and the coughing got worse. Much worse.

Janie screamed. She was swimming all right, but she was screaming. My head was buzzing, but I could hear she was calling for her mother. I determined to keep up my head and stop the coughing. I knew I had to stop the coughing. I took a breath and held it. Then I gradually let the air out. I could hear Alice calling now but I was not certain what she said. Janie was still screaming, but after Alice called she ceased. I heard Alice's overarm coming toward me. She was swimming the wrong way. It would not do.

My head got clearer now and the coughing ceased. The

196

tickle was still in my chest, but if I was careful with the breathing I could keep from coughing.

Janie was crying as she swam in little strokes. Alice came up.

Janie said, "Daddy's coughing. Why don't they come? Mamma, help me."

Alice put a hand under her.

"They'll come soon, honey." She put her other hand under my back and said, "Don't try to talk, Sam. Float awhile and it will get better."

I said, "Take Janie on. How's Pete?"

"He's okay. He's floating awhile."

Janie was still crying.

Alice and I were looking at each other.

I said, "Go, darling. I'll follow. Feel better each minute. How about you?"

I put my hand under her back now. We each had a hand under the other's back and she had Janie with her other hand.

She said, "I can make it. Oh, Sam!"

"Quit that. Now go, darling. Take her to Pete. Then take them along easy. I'll catch you soon."

We looked at each other again. A long look.

Then she said, "Yes, Sam dear. Come soon, dear."

"I will."

She said, "Come, Janie," and started to swim with her, holding her with one hand.

I lay on my back and floated some. I felt better. I started to swim. As I started to swim I felt better still. The tickle had gone now from my chest.

I caught up with Alice and Janie. We all three of us caught up with Pete. Pete was looking rested. Alice smiled at me.

Janie said, "I wish they'd come. I wish they'd come."

From across the lake came the sudden roar of the motor of the speedboat.

I saw the fear in Pete's eyes and in Alice's eyes.

Pete said, "They saw us! When they were riding up they looked back. I knew they looked back. Just when they got to the trees."

Janie said, "They're coming back. My good, my good!"

Alice said, "What now, Sam?"

I said, "Let's say a prayer."

Janie said, "What for? It isn't bedtime."

Pete said, "What prayer shall we say, Dad?"

Alice said, "We'll say, 'Our Father.'"

We were all close together now. The roar of the motor was increasing. I could see the white wedge, the bow high in the air like before. We started saying the prayer together. There was nothing else to do. Maybe it was better this way. This way it would be quicker. We would all go together this way, not one by one.

"'Hallowed be Thy Name. Thy kingdom come. Thy will be done, in earth as it is in heaven. Give us this day our daily bread. . . .'"

It was coming very fast. It looked so beautiful from the water line. It was still far away, but it was getting bigger and more beautiful all the time.

"'As we forgive them that trespass against us. And lead us not into temptation; But deliver us from evil.'"

Deliver us from evil. It would not be long now. The evil and the trespass. Forgive the trespass that delivered us from the evil. Alice's eyes were very blue. Alice's eyes were as blue as the sky. Pete was steadier now. Janie was saying the words like a parrot. Just because we were saying them. Her eyes were excitedly watching the boat. It was getting close now. It would not be long now. I would see that Janie never knew. I would make it quick for her, the last

198

thing I would do. Alice's eyes were so blue. They were as blue as the sky.

"'For thine is the kingdom, the power and the glory, for ever and ever. Amen.'"

The roar was tremendous now. He was coming straight for us. Straight for the little close bunch of us. This way would be best of all. It would just smash in and that was it. Better than cat and mouse play, prodding with boat-hooks and things, better than that. Speed was mercy. Friday had the quality of mercy. The quality of mercy is not strained. The quality of mercy. Alice and I looked at each other. She knew their purpose too. She was saying good-by. With her dear eyes. Suddenly the motor slowed.

We looked back at the boat. They were going to do it the other way after all. Now I could see the bridge, now that the bow was down in the water. There was only one man on the bridge. He was not wearing a blue shirt. He was not wearing a black and white check shirt. He was wearing a business suit.

He called out, "Hold on, folks. I'll get you in."

It was Mason Brown.

13

He brought the boat up very slow, reversing his propeller as he came close, then idling the motor so that the boat lay drifting beside us. He threw a rope ladder over the side and I handed the kids up to him, Janie first and then Pete.

Then I got Alice up. She was trembling all over now, and very white in the face, with her hair streaking down around her, and her body was very cold and I knew she could not have gone much farther, not Alice even. She was only wearing her bra and panties and I found some blankets in the locker and gave her one, while Mason Brown wrapped up the children; then I found one for myself and we all lay down on the deck like a row of cordwood and nobody said a word, while he went back to the wheel and circled around and headed back for the boathouse. At least I presumed he did that, but for all I knew or cared right at that moment he might have been heading for the moon. By the time we got back to the boathouse we were beginning to catch hold of ourselves a little.

There were some towels in the boathouse. We dried ourselves and wrapped the blankets around us again and got in his car. He had a black Ford sedan. Alice and the children got in the back and I got in the front with him. He started the motor and began driving up the bumpy track.

We passed our horses all still tied up where we had left them.

I said, "Did you get Oakes and Friday?"

He shook his head.

"Mrs. Oakes was there alone. I introduced myself and the other agent with me as friends of yours. She told us you were up here. I left him there to look around and came up here fast on a hunch."

I said, "It was certainly lucky for us. We were about done."

He brushed it off.

"What happened?"

I gave him a complete chronological report of everything that had happened from the moment we had arrived at the ranch, even including the blotting paper which now rested at the bottom of the lake in my coat pocket. It took a long time. By the end of it we had come to the fork. Friday's and Johnny's horses were tied to a tree. The Jaguar was gone. But our car was still there.

"Thank God," Alice said. "Now we will be able to get clothes."

Mason Brown thought a minute.

He said, "The trouble is, that if you take your car or clothes from it they will know you survived."

Alice stared at him.

"Are you suggesting that we —"

He cut in.

"I guess not." He sighed. "In that case I'll have to close in on them right away." He turned to me. "Can you change fast and come to the inn with me?"

Alice said, "Why do you need him any more, Mr. Mason Brown?"

He said, "To point them out to me. I'm sorry, Mrs. Freeman. Do you think you feel well enough to drive after us when you are ready and meet your husband at the inn?"

"I suppose so," she said.

She awakened Janie, who had been sleeping like a baby all the way down. Pete had been listening to every word.

He said, "Can I come with you, Mr. Mason Brown? Please let me come with you. I can change just as fast as my dad can. Quicker."

He said, "But we'll need you to be a bodyguard to your mother and sister."

"They don't need one."

Alice said, "Come on, son."

We all got changed and I kissed Alice.

She said, "Sam, be careful. Please."

I kissed her again.

"Take it easy. I'm only going to point them out. See you there, huh?"

She didn't like it, and I didn't like leaving her that way, but I had to. I got my gun out of my car and got in Mason Brown's car again and we drove off down the right-hand track to the highway. We did not talk all the way to Santa Serena.

When we got to the town, I showed him where the inn was on the corner joining the coast highway. He swung into the parking lot. There were a lot of cars in it, but I could not see the Jaguar.

"There's the tourists' bus," I said. "So the lunch is still going on. They should be here."

"There's a Jaguar behind that sedan," he said. "That his?"

I looked.

"Yes," I said. "That's it. They're still here."

"Good. I want to grab them before they get back to the ranch. I see you have a gun there. In case it's necessary, I guess you remember how to use it?"

"I remember."

We went in the inn, and could not see them around. The tourists had broken up their lunch at the long table and were wandering out, looking very silly with their souvenirs and their cans of soup. The women had stickpins and the men had redwood ashtrays with Santa Serena written on them, and they all looked a little self-conscious. I thought of asking them if they had seen where Johnny had gone, but then I saw Max and asked him if he'd seen Johnny and Steve.

Max said, "I don't know, maybe they're in the men's room, Mr. Freeman, if they haven't left already. Is this gentleman with you Mr. Mason Brown?"

"That's right."

Max said, "You are to call a Mr. Gaines at the Oakes ranch. He said it was urgent."

Mason Brown said, "Thanks." He turned to me. "You look for them and hold them while I call Gaines."

"Right."

Max took him to the back office to call. I looked around. They were not at any of the little tables in the other lunch-room. They were not in the bar. I crossed the bar and went into the men's room. As I went in, I had my gun at the ready. They were both in the men's room. Alone.

They were just on their way out as I went in. You should have seen their faces. You should have seen them. They put up their hands fast enough.

Johnny said, "Well, I'll be!"

Friday said, "You damn fool! I told you we should have made sure."

But he wasn't speaking to me, although he was looking at me. He was speaking to Johnny.

I said, "All right, come on out, and make it slow."

I started to back toward the door. They started to move slowly across the room.

Johnny said, "Of all things, a stick-up in a place like this. A stick-up!"

He was speaking to me, but I knew it didn't make sense. And I had seen his eyes flick over my shoulder. At once I realized someone had come into the room behind me. There was no time to explain it was not a stick-up. I ducked fast to avoid the man behind me. At the same time I jumped to the side wall to take in all three of them. As I ducked and jumped, Friday kicked hard at my right hand. There was a shooting pain in my right hand. I dropped the gun. There was no other man in the room at all. I had fallen for the oldest gag in the world.

They both jumped me together. I got in a quick, hard jab at Johnny's stomach and he doubled up. At the same time Friday must have hit me on the head. I went down. I went down with my body over the gun. I could feel the gun under my ribs as I fell on it, but I could not move to get it. I could not move at all.

Vaguely, through the blur in my head, I saw Friday grab at Johnny, jerk him up. They ran out together before I could move. It must have taken me a full sixty seconds to move at all. I got my hand on the gun. Then I managed to get to my feet. My hand hurt like hell, but I held the gun with it because I needed my left hand to open the door. I got the door open and ran out into the lobby and across the lobby and down the steps into the parking lot outside. My head began to clear a little as I hit the fresh air out in the parking lot and I looked around for them but I couldn't see them anywhere. The Jaguar was still there. The other cars were still there. The tourists' bus was moving off down the highway. Pete was running across the parking lot toward me.

204

"Dad, Dad! Quick, they got in the bus!"

"Okay, where's the car?"

"We're in the gas station across the street. There's a police car here. Look."

I saw the highway patrol car just across the lot. I ran to tell them. Pete ran with me. When I got to the car it was empty. There was nobody in it at all. I looked around for the cops and couldn't see them anywhere.

The bus was disappearing down the coast highway. The keys were left in the patrol car. I opened the door and got in and pressed the starter. I said, "Tell them I've gone to stop the bus."

I saw the cops come out of the diner as I started up. I moved off as they ran out in the road. I heard the rear door of the car slam and looked round. Pete was sitting in the back seat.

He said, "Dad, can I work the siren?"

There wasn't time to stop. Hardly propitious now.

"You little fool! Okay, climb over."

He climbed over into the front seat beside me. His eyes were shining. "Why did they get in the bus, Dad? Why didn't they take the Jag?"

"The Jag's a marked car. Nobody would think of them escaping in a tourists' bus."

We were gaining on the bus. I could see it now way down the highway. I looked for the siren button.

Pete said, "That's the siren, there, Dad. Can I work it?"

"Go ahead."

He switched it on. The siren began to wail. I turned on the red spot.

The bus was pulling over to the side.

I said, "Now you sit tight, son. No more monkey business. Understand?"

"Yes, Dad."

I pulled up in front of the bus and got out. I had the gun in my left hand. I could shoot Friday and Johnny just as well with my left hand anyway.

The driver opened the door and looked inquiringly at me. I said, "I want those two men who just got in."

He looked back at me blankly.

"Which two men do you mean, sir?"

I looked down the bus. Every seat was filled. And Johnny and Friday were not there. I looked at them all carefully. Men and women. Not one of them remotely resembled Johnny or Friday. They were all looking at me in varying degrees of astonishment.

I turned back to the driver.

I said, "Didn't two men jump in just as you were pulling out of the parking lot back there?"

He looked as blank as before, looked around at the passengers. He said, "I got the same passengers I had from L.A. as far as I can see. Any of you folks got any strangers next to you who weren't here before?"

They all looked around at each other, a little apprehensively, looked back at me.

I said, "You folks remember the man who gave you the soup at lunchtime? He and another man? Didn't he get on this bus?"

A woman said, "Oh, I saw them just as we were leaving. They ran around the side of the bus and got in a car and drove off."

A man sitting a couple of rows behind her said, "That's right. I saw them too. They drove off just ahead of us."

"What kind of car was it?" I asked.

"Blue sedan. I didn't take notice what kind it was, mister."

I was beginning to feel very foolish. Very foolish indeed.

I said, "Anyone else see this car?"

Another man said, "I saw a blue Cadillac pull out. I didn't see who got in it."

"Which way did it go?"

"Down the road ahead of us, same way as us."

"Anyone get the license number?"

Nobody had.

I turned back to the driver.

"Okay, driver, I guess there's been a mistake. Thank you."

He muttered something.

I got out and went back to the car and got in and turned around and headed back to the inn. I couldn't go chasing a blue Cadillac without a number.

Pete said, "What happened, Dad? Why didn't you get them?"

"Listen, son. Did you actually see them get into the bus?"

"Yes, Dad. I saw them run around the bus to get in."

"You mean you were at the other side of the door of the bus?"

"That's right. But I saw them go around. I saw them distinctly."

"They didn't get in the bus, son. They ran around and got in another car."

"Are you sure, Dad? Are you sure they weren't on the bus?"

"Of course I'm sure."

"Did you look behind all the seats?"

"Don't be silly, boy. Do you suppose neither the driver nor any one of the passengers would have seen them?"

He said, "Well, what kind of a car was it they got in?"

"A blue Cadillac, pulled out just ahead of the bus."

"I didn't see a blue Cadillac."

"You should keep your eyes open, boy."

He began to cry. I knew I shouldn't have bawled him

out, but my hand was hurting and I could see the cops standing in the parking lot waiting as I drove up. Mason Brown was standing with them. So were Alice and Janie.

I pulled up by them and Pete and I got out. They were all looking in the car.

"What happened?" Mason Brown said.

One of the cops said, "Couldn't you catch that bus?"

I said, "I caught the bus but they weren't on it. They got a blue Cadillac parked next the bus. Pete here made a mistake."

Alice said, "Blue Cadillac, nuts. I saw them climb into the bus myself."

I said, "You and Pete couldn't see the door side of the bus, hon."

"Pete couldn't. He was by the car. But I could. I was bringing Janie out of the rest room and from there I could see them get in the door. Who said anything about a blue Cadillac anyway?"

I stared at her, at them all. They were all staring at me.

I said, "All the passengers did. And the driver didn't see them get in either. They must all be in cahoots together! The whole lot of them!"

Mason Brown turned to the cops.

"I want that bus held. And I want every man and woman on it held. Every one of them is a spy. Hop to it."

The cops looked at each other.

One said, "Gaviota?"

The other looked at his watch, nodded.

"That'll give them plenty. Springer Special bus, tell Mike."

"Best make it a blanket roadblock all busses, huh? Case there's another Springer maybe?"

"Okay. I'll come and talk to Mike too."

208

They ran off together toward the public telephone booth in the corner of the lot.

Pete said, "I told you, Dad."

Alice said, "Be quiet, son."

A station wagon drove into the lot. Liza was driving. Her face was white. A man in a business suit was sitting beside her. He looked very grave.

Mason Brown said, "There's Gaines now."

I said, "What did he say on the phone?"

"He'd left already. We'll soon find out what he's got."

They got out and came toward us. He was carrying something in his hands. It was a can of Serena Soup. He was carrying it very carefully, in both hands.

Mason Brown walked to meet them. I went with him.

Gaines said, "See this?" He held it up carefully. I saw that one end was slightly different from the other. Only slightly, but it was different. When you looked at it closely you could see there was a join. It was a screw top.

Gaines said, "When you turn this lid, it's armed. It has a fifteen minute fuse. I examined them up at the ranch. There are five cases up there. Forty-four in each case."

Mason Brown said, "What's the explosive?"

Gaines glanced at me and at Liza.

He said, "You'll know the name, George. It's our latest. If you recall, it's supposed to be top secret."

Mason Brown whistled.

"Where did you find them?"

"In the shed." He put the can down carefully on the ground and took something out of his pocket. "I found this too. In his bedroom."

It was a small oilskin pouch, very small, with a zipper on it. He unzipped it, took out a couple of sheets of paper. They were typewritten lists of names and addresses. The addresses were from all over the country. They were all key spots. They were marked off in six groups.

"There are forty-four in each group," he said.

Against each group there was a date. The first group was marked with today's date.

"And forty-four seats on the bus," I said. "That's it. Friday swam ashore with this master list. There's a bus coming in each day this week. Those were the people he was writing to. To come to L.A. and catch the busses."

Mason Brown said, "Wasn't there one yesterday?"

"Yes, last night. It was the first one Johnny tried it with. But he took that soup from the restaurant. That must have been an innocent one. To make sure Max would go for it. I remember Johnny said he would try it for just one week, using his own sample cans. That's the six busses including today's being the first."

Mason Brown wheeled.

"What are those patrolmen doing?"

They were coming away from the phone booth, running toward us.

"The bus didn't arrive through Gaviota, sir. So we called the Richfield Service station at the turn off to the San Marcos Pass. It went up there fifteen minutes ago. They must have been suspicious."

The other said, "If we take this Santa Ynez route we can maybe catch him about the top of the San Marcos."

Mason Brown said, "That bus is full of enough explosive to blow the whole pass to hell, officer. Call Santa Barbara. Have them send out all the men they can lay hands on. Have them meet that bus as she comes down the coast side of the pass. Warn them to be careful. Whatever they do they must not cause that bus to wreck. That stuff is not too stable."

They looked at him.

One of them said, "In that case, we'd best have the whole route closed to all traffic, hadn't we, sir?"

"Guess you'd better."

They ran back to the phone booth.

Liza was looking at me.

She said, "You knew, Sam! You knew and you didn't tell me."

I couldn't bear the way she was looking at me.

"Liza, dear Liza. I wasn't allowed to tell you."

She looked at Mason Brown, back to me.

"I guess not. I'm the wife of a spy, aren't I? I'm the wife of a spy."

"Liza. You couldn't know, my dear. You couldn't help it."

Her eyes went hard.

"Where's Johnny now? Where are they both?"

"They're on the bus with the others."

She nodded slowly.

"And then he'll be sent to jail for so many years and then he'll be let out for good behavior and then —" She broke off. She began to laugh. It was a terrible laugh, terrible.

Mason Brown was looking at her. He started to say something, changed his mind. He was out of his depth.

I put my arms around her.

"Liza, Alice and I will take you home with us. You'll be all right, dear, you'll be all right."

She stopped laughing suddenly. She grew calm. It was a steel calm. She said, "Of course I'll be all right." She took her bag from under her arm, took out a pack of cigarettes.

"Light me one, will you, Sam?"

I lit her cigarette. We looked in each other's eyes. Her eyes were glistening a little, like the water she painted, they were.

She said, "Thanks." Her eyes focused over my shoulder.

"Look," she said. "There's the bus coming back now. It didn't go over the San Marcos at all. Look!"

We both turned and looked. We looked down the highway as far as we could see. There was no bus.

We turned back to her. She was gone. She was already in the Jaguar across the lot. We ran toward her. The car roared, shot out of our reach just as we got up to her.

"Liza! Don't do it! Don't do it, Liza!"

It was no good. She couldn't have heard me anyway. Not above the roar of that motor. She must have been doing forty before she shifted from low to second. Possibly forty-five. On the road to Santa Ynez. On the road to the San Marcos Pass.

Mason Brown said, "Confound it! We've got to catch her." He started to sprint toward his car. He yelled, "Gaines! Alert headquarters."

I ran with Mason Brown, jumped in beside him. I saw Alice and the children running toward us.

I called to her.

"Honey, you stay right here! I'll be back."

We were out of the lot and going up the road. Mason Brown said, "You may not be back at that if we don't catch her."

I said, "We'll never catch her in that car. She's the best damn driver in the country is my guess."

I remembered Johnny's words as he went around that corner at seventy. 'Liza can beat it herself when she's in the mood.'

She was in the mood. Already she was out of sight over the rise ahead, past the edge of the town. When we got there we could see the valley ahead of us. And we could see Liza. The road was straight as a die. For miles it went

212

straight, direct for the pass at the head of the valley. And that Jaguar must have been doing a hundred and thirty.

"If she hits the intersections at that speed —" He didn't finish his sentence.

I said, "She will. Odds are in her favor at that speed. There's little traffic on them anyway."

He asked, "Where does the other road join in, the one the bus is on?"

"About a mile below the pass. It'll be by there about now. My guess is she should catch it about halfway up."

"Are there many houses in the pass country?"

"Not on this side. Not like the coast side. This side is as wild as Death Valley."

"Let's pray she hits it this side then. Those mountains will absorb most of it."

I looked at him.

"You know she will, huh?"

"Don't you?"

I said, "Yes. I know she will. There's nothing on God's earth can stop her."

We didn't talk any more. He drove on, as fast as he could. We were doing ninety-five. That was as fast as the car would go. And we might as well have been standing still, as far as catching Liza was concerned. There was a complete feeling of futility. And yet also, strangely, I felt an inner calm.

I thought of all the things I knew about Liza. All the moments I had seen her. They were very few, the moments I had known Liza, and yet, somehow, they seemed now to be like a lifetime. . . .

"Here, Jilly girl, come now, here Jilly."
"That her name, Jilly?"
"Her name's Black Jill really, but we call her Jilly."
"What's your name?"

"Me? Oh, I'm Liza."

"I'm going to breed Jill to Mark in another three years."

"Sounds like you might get a crazy horse to me."

"Double your chances of all the good or all the bad."

"Suppose it turns out the other way?"

"I can have it shot."

"All right, so you just got back from the war. You think I didn't guess that the moment I saw you?"

"Quit that, Mark. Quit that stuff."

"Any time you need a job, you're hired."

"Were you in Africa?"

"Little time, yes."

"You didn't get to Abyssinia did you?"

"No. Why?"

"I just wondered. I knew some people who were lost there once."

"What do we do next?"

"What do you suggest, Johnny?"

"We'll fix the tank together. You get the supper."

"Yes, Johnny."

Yes Johnny, no Johnny, yes Johnny.

"No saffron today, Lizakin?"

"Last time you had too much saffron even though I only put in a pinch. You said it spoiled the wine flavor. So this time I put in orégano and sweet basil and rosemary."

"And garlic."

"Yes, Johnny, and pepper and salt. Can you taste that too, maybe?"

"Sometimes, of course, a dish can become too spicy, Lizakin."

"Oh, Dad. I'm sorry you don't like it."

"Of course I like it."

"His name is Sam."

"He has not the farm in his blood."

"I guess that's right. I'll end up in the city. But the farm is good for a change."

"Liza can take you up, can't you, Liza? After all, it's your lake."

214

"He means I like to paint it. It's very lovely."

"You paint too? I'd like to see some."

"Banana custard, your favorite, Dad."

"I always like to put a coat on when I go out. It makes me seem more like a lady and less like a farmer."

"Did Dad tell you why he adopted me?"

"I can remember my father and mother, but not my brother very well. He was away at school a lot and I was just a kid."

"Did Dad tell you why he adopted me?"

"I'm so worried about him, Sam. Did he say anything to you about his health?"

"Now it's your turn to go through the mill. Why don't you have a girl?"

"What's her name?"

"You've got a girl, you're not with her, you're all confused up. From the moment I see you, you are. Tell Momma."

"Good-by, Sam dear, and give Alice my love."

We were beginning the climb now. The road was beginning to curve and twist and we had to drop a lot of speed. We had passed the road where the bus would have joined in, and now we were in the desolate land at the foot of the pass. At each bend I looked across the twist of the rocky gorge, up and across to see if Liza was on any of the upper reaches. And then I saw the bus.

It was way up, going very slowly, maybe two thousand feet up, and although it was perhaps only a mile or so away as the crow flies, it must have been four or five by the road, almost to the summit of the pass. There was an uninterrupted view across the gorge of the ribbon of the road as it took the long gradual curve before disappearing again into the mountain.

Mason Brown stopped the car.

He said, "If she doesn't catch it there —"

"Listen."

215

In the silence of the mountain, now that our own motor was ceased, you could hear the whine of the bus quite distinctly as it crawled up the gradient, and you could hear too, though muffled by the angle of the defile, the pulsating throb of the Jaguar, somewhere down below, still out of our sight.

I said, "She's getting close now. I think she's —"

"There!" he pointed. "She's still on the lower curve. She'll never make it."

Even as he spoke the black Jaguar flashed out of sight again, into the final bend before emerging to the upper stretch. We waited. We waited. The bus was halfway along its open stretch now, before Liza finally appeared.

And then there was no doubt about it any more. I do not know if the bus driver could hear her above his own motor or not. In any case he was completely vulnerable. He had to keep on the outside of the road, the side of the precipice, or risk some oncoming car.

She took the risk. She swept up at him on the left, like a black torpedo, and then we couldn't see her any more as she passed inside, between him and the rock. She must have aimed straight for his left front wheel. At any rate the bus swerved violently out, seemed to hang for a moment, then fell, down the mountain. The last I saw, the tiny body of the Jaguar shot out over him, out into space, spinning wildly in the air.

Mason Brown had yanked me by the arm, pulling me out of the car, into the inside ditch at the side of the road. We covered our heads with our arms.

It was not long in coming. I remember that. It was not long in coming. And then I did not remember any more.

14

Someone was sobbing, and I lay cradled in her arms. I was still in the ditch, and I looked up and saw Alice was crying as she bent over me.

I said, "I told you to stay. I told you to stay."

"That was some time ago, Sam. Are you all right, Sam?"

"Of course I'm all right. Just the blast I guess. I didn't duck fast enough. Where's Mason Brown?"

"He's all right. He's down at the fire."

I could smell the smoke now. I had thought it was a cigarette. But it was the fire in the gorge.

"Is it bad? I'd better go down and help."

"No such thing. They've got it almost out now."

"You shouldn't have driven here."

"I didn't drive, Sam. I came in one of the fire trucks. That's how we're going back, unless you need an ambulance?"

"What about Mason Brown's car?"

"You should see it!"

"Where are the children?"

"I left them at the inn."

I looked at Alice. Her eyes were blue.

I said, "Liza sent you her love."